THE GRAVITY HARP

Crewless, with warm tea still swirling in abandoned cups, The Mary Celeste arrives in Gibraltar, December 5, 1872.

THE GRAVITY HARP
A Novella

by
BULL GARLINGTON

CREATIVE WRITER PRO
2018
CHICAGO

Creative Writer PRO
6727 North Ionia Avenue
Chicago, Illinois 60646
www.creativewriter.pro

Ordering Information:
Quantity sales. Special discounts are available on quantity purchases by corporations, associations, and others. For details, contact the publisher at the address above.
Orders by U.S. trade bookstores and wholesalers.

Printed in the United States of America

Publisher's Cataloging-in-Publication data
Garlington, Christopher "Bull"
The Gravity Harp / Bull Garlington
ISBN 978-1-6425460-5-7
1. Literature–Science Fiction–Novellas.

Preface

This novella is presented in the order in which it was written. This is abnormal, but it is how the story fell out of my head. Most writers who write this way go back and fix the damn thing in post, which is smart and maybe I should have done that so you, dear reader, experience a story that unfolds in linear time.

But, where would be the fun in that?

FOREWORD

I don't know about other Science Fiction writers but sometimes I think I can't write fast enough to keep up with new technology and culture.

Since I started writing this story, some of the technology has come on line. Only a few years ago, there were no driverless cars. Drone delivery was not a thing. Artificial Intelligence was only in the movies. Augemented Reality was clunkish at best. But then, it was pretty obvious they were on the way. However, I could not have believed they would arrive so quickly.

EULOGY

[From Double Kurzweil News stream]

The biggest question is, of course: who killed the bicycle king? Found slumped in the swinging chair of his self-propelled gypsy camion, William Yeats Butler died of electrical shock. This is most intriguing, as Mr. Butler, aka, the Bicycle King, was virtually allergic to electricity.

Butler had lived most of his adult life on the road. On his Portuguese tax record, under occupation, Butler had most recently claimed "philosopher." This is easy to comprehend if you'd ever met Butler: his post-tech mannerisms, his fondness for a pipe, his spectacles. If you were making a movie about Wittgenstein, Butler would play the lead. He was whip thin, could tie himself into yogic knots, and grew his own vegetables in found bottles tied to the infamous vehicle, his nom de rig, what Butler called home and the rest of us called the Merry Celeste.

It is difficult to accurately portray the vehicle Butler had created. If you're reading this article, you probably linked here from a picture of it. I'll try, but having seen it in person, I can tell you this: side A might not be the same after you've worked your way around to side B, C, D, E and back. There was too much detail, too much organic mass, for it to ever remain the same.

The Merry Celeste:

Imagine a gothic and ornate complicated piece of rattan furniture, something singular and Victorian. Wicker so thin it seems more like gauze yet nearly strong as steel. Butler said it was all bamboo and hemp with some organic shellac he whipped up on the spot in the summer when he was bored and needed to patch holes.

Now imagine this wicker furniture has dreamed up a wicker conservatory formerly grafted to the belly of a steampunk Zeppelin. Now, onto all of that, somehow, splice an Amish buggy front-end to a chassis made from a bicycle as hallucinated by an overachieving octopus with a fondness for Chiti Chiti Bang Bang and gears. A summer hearse designed by Roger Dean.

Now drape the exterior with rain catchers and potted plants, with copper tubing, flowers, strange reels of hemp stems, bowers of wicker branches, automatic collapsible cane fishing poles, extendable micro sails, kites, a birdcage with a fat sleepy chicken, beautiful hand-lettered signs (some that make sense and advertise: Storyteller! Some that make none: Beware of Ninjas!) From the top of the wagon, two spinning pillars: rotating sails that harness the wind no matter the direction, delivering it to a massive collection of coiled kevlar springs and cogs located beneath the carriage.

Inside the belly of the whale: Butler's office, his library, and his hammock chair. A handful of cut glass bottles stuffed into a nest of scarves, filled with amber liquids. A banjo. An apothecary of soap bubble bottles. A shrink-wrapped brick of 33-004 8¼ x 6 7/8 inch spiral notebooks. A Ziploc bag of .07 black sharpies ziplined to a bamboo rafter. A deck of pornographic tarot cards. Balloons.

Now imagine this cacophony traveling the highways and byways of the Americas under sail, ticking along like a broom closet making tired love to a calliope. On that front bench, in a weird hat and wrap-around shades, W. Y. Butler, a.k.a., "the Bicycle King," a plume of English Witch tobacco trailing behind him, the sticks and levers of his engineering miracle jarring his loose grip as his contraption moved along even in the lightest breezes.

I once passed The Merry Celeste as it crept up a long hill outside Los Cruces, N.M. It moved so slow, so barely. As I finally came around, taking advantage of a break in traffic, I saw Butler wasn't even steering. He was reading a book.

Butler would stop on a whim. He'd find a place that suited him and just decamp. No one ever complained. No broken ordinances were ever levied over his arrival. He could park in front of a fire hydrant and the fire department would invite him in for lunch. He would stop, and The Merry Celeste, having stored energy all day, at the gentle urging of a few carefully pulled levers, would settle, would withdraw its sails, would lower the steps at its caboose and ignite the sodium lanterns swinging on the back porch. A black canvas awning would slowly unravel and drop its flaps upon which were written in white blatant script the actions Butler might perform if moved to do so. The most famous of these flaps, that small bunting-sized flense that fell like bangs over the entrance to his cart has baffled children from Columbia to Kennebunkport. It's not the Voiynich manuscript, but I still know a couple of real estate salesmen who think it has magical powers. Maybe they're right. I'll leave you with it, an epitaph if you will, for this remarkable man:

Hew Hobe Lie
Ves Muchex Perie
Ncesm Uch

NAMES

\<most common girl's name\>
Aya
\<commonest united states female given name ranked\>
Mary 2.508 million
Jennifer 1.543 million
\<commonest united states surname\>
Smith 2.376 million
\<commonest city name\>
Franklin (32)
Clinton (27)
\<commonest occupation\>
Food service technician

WANDER

[Mary Jennifer Jones] has found the perfect place. In a room added onto the back of a tricked out double-wide in the Orange Court trailer park in Franklin, Florida. There is no stream. No jack. No phone. No wifi. No Nub. No Sweet Maria's coffee bodega. No Bluetooth. Grid maintenance hasn't gone far enough back in time to reach the particular wasted weekend of 1974 into which this trailer park once crashed; power comes over electric cables as thick as her wrist. The magnetic signature looks like fireworks. Most searches skip right over it. [Mary Jennifer Jones]'s landlord is a trustafarian reject with a deep hatred for tech. His ganja is prime. His habits are predictable. His no-tech policy is strict, overbearing, and trends about four trailers deep in every direction. [Mary Jennifer Jones]'s room, should it be viewed from above, sits dead center in the least electronically detectable zone in America and she is fucking proud.

[Jennifer Jones]'s multi is stored safely away in a leather pouch stuffed into a wad of t-shirts currently under debate as to their efficacy in expressing both her decidedly anti-capitalist trendencies and her morbid dread of stepping outside the bubble of magnetic skew in which she now resides.

In order to find her, someone would have to think. They'd have to make some kind of leap of intuition, some kind of massive glurch, they'd have to initiate an Aha moment, point their finger to the sky and determine: *we need to look not for an individual, not for a unique signature, not for Darja Zieliechs, a unique name, but for Mary, for Jennifer, the most common name. For Jones.* Who do you become when you disappear? You don't become Dweezil Zappa. You become Mary Smith. You don't become another individual—you become a group. You become the most possible. Instead of being nowhere, you're everywhere. And where do you live? New York? Tarrington? Google? No. You live in Clinton, on Main Street, in apartment 212. You're a nurse. You own a thirteen-year-old grey Toyota 4-door sedan with a bumper sticker that says "My kid's on the Honor roll!" with manual steering.

You'd have to decide to stop tracing her brush (the tendency of people to trace their fingers over their pads in the exact same manner, no matter what they're doing). Easier to track than a fingerprint. And built-in.

You'd have to stop the voiceprint trace.

You'd have to stop looking for purchase patterns.

You'd have to stop looking.

[Jones] does not want to be found. She has no pad. She has no phone. She has no car. She buys everything with cash cards. She has no plastic.

She is a nurse in Franklin. She is a cashier at the mall. She is the toll-booth operator up the turnpike. She is the sound tech for the New Life church. She is black. She is Indian. She is Filipino. She speaks with an accent. She curses in Tagalog. She lies in perfect English.

You can't find her. Because you are looking for her. And she will. Not. Be found.

Music

[Blue October: "Into the Ocean"]
Tosh: What're we listening to.
[Jones]: Stuff I don't listen to.
Tosh: Heh.
[Jones]: I mean, I don't usually listen to this.
Tosh: I don't know. . .
[Jones]: Yah. True.
Tosh: Poppy. I like it. Makes me happy.
[Jones]: Are you listening to the lyrics?
Tosh: Yeah, but they're an Irish band. I can't understand a single word.
[laughter]
[Jones]: Toshy!
[The Elizabeth Dane: *Skeletal Sounds*]
[Jones]: Legacy.
Tosh: I like it. The mood.
[Jones]: Got to love the lyrics.
Tosh: They still walk among us.
[Jones]: Did you ever see that movie, "They Live"?
Tosh: Legacy.
[Jones]: You can't use that word. You're NT.
Tosh: Not tall?
[Jones]: Non tech. That's tech jargon: legacy. Older than dirt; leftover from several versions previous. Unusable.

Tosh: I got that. Nomenclature. I love it. But I have my own and I try not to employ the current fad for compression.

[Jones]: That's exactly what it is. Compression. Check it.

[Jones] pulls a Sharpie out of her shirt pocket with a brown board pad. She writes:

=X=

Tosh: Shorthand?

[Jones]: "Is what it is."

Tosh: Gematria. All language is like that when you break it down. Letters for sounds. Sounds for emotions. Words are just encapsulated emotions strung together to make short hand meanings. None of the words we use today mean what they actually mean. Especially in English. It's all trash magic. Abused code.

[Jones]: I can see that.

Tosh: So a word is already a compression. I mean, take compression. Break it down. Co is a latinate prefix for together, press is garbage latin that means kind of the same thing as *prise* or *pull apart*. Only the co in front of it tells you that it's reversed so you're pulling or pushing things together. Ion is just a garbage ending from when English, German, and Nordic were all fighting over diction. Pirate verbiage. If we uncompress this, it says: *the bringing of things together with force.* That's a lot of mouth. So we compress it and say compress. If we didn't do that, we'd spend most of our lives just saying hello.

[Jones]: So you like tech jargon?

Tosh: Oh hell no, girl. I like my verbiage like I like my women. Voluptuous and complicated.

[laughter]

[Jones]: I'm afraid I don't meet the criteria.

Tosh: It's a general preference. I'm open to variation.

[Jones]: Let's table that.

Tosh: Ooh, corp speak.

[Jones]: Put the overture down!

Tosh: Cop speak!

[Jones]: That dog won't hunt.

Tosh: Cracker!

[Jones]: AFK.

Tosh: Chat room let down.

[Jones]: What the fool believes.

Tosh: Ah, now. Uncalled for. Bringing Steely Dan into the mix. Treading on sacred ground, sweets.

[Jones]: Sorry.

Tosh: Man's got to put his cards on the table.

[Jones]: I'm flattered. But, I'm busy.

Tosh: Well, in the meantime, perhaps we can put a dent into this donculous Tupperware full of robust and mystical ganja.

[Jones]: Ahh gaaad. How can we do any more!?

Tosh: There's no upper limit my dear.

[Tosh rises. The walls of his trailer are lined floor to ceiling with books, movies, knick knacks. He disappears down the hallway. Comes back carrying a big cardboard box with a picture of a fan on it. He pulls a leather coated Stereoptical viewfinder out of the case and pours the contents of the box onto the shag carpet floor between them: hundreds of black & white cards with duplicate pictures of World War I, zeppelins, catastrophe, Victorian gardens, palaces. When [Jones] looks through the device, the pictures have spooky depth. They go through them for most of the night.]

Triple Word Score

Chicago's Illinois Masonic Long Term Care Facility is a sprawling assemblage of micro hospitals depending away from an older, original structure. In the basement of a farthest wing is the information desaturation room. Z is visiting the hospital as an investor and has asked to see this particular chamber.

"In my home country, it is a problem. Some people fall asleep with their faces on their tabla. Some have waterproof cases so they can update from the shower. I saw a guy in the other end of your hospital fighting with the nurses who wanted to hold his scroll while he was scanned. It's like that everywhere. And the advertising; look," Ziechlech waves his hand in front of the elevator. The doors open, he beckons everyone in. The walls are glass. Once the doors close, the walls disappear and the group finds themselves floating gently through the aisles of the very hospital they're in. A voice over tells the story of Illinois Masonic. "This morning in my hotel, I took a bath in field of flowers that were all shaped like the logo for Havalac Dairy. It was disconcerting. The warning grooves leading up to the departures gate at Dulles yesterday, they made the wheels of our car whisper 'British Petroleum supports Virginia's Coalition for Energy Savings'. The tires told me this."

The group steps out of the elevator, back into the hallway. Ziechlech walks up to the portal for the desaturation chamber and empties his pockets. He places several items onto a black velvet-lined tray as a clerk arranges them for a photographic record.

"My live pen, which records everything I write and takes a picture whenever I sign my name so I can prove it was me who signed. My pad, this little obsidian lozenge, which can do, as far as I can tell, anything. It is my camera, my phone, my bank, my personal assistant, my defender, a beacon . . . My frames, which show me an augmented reality and real time stats about my company. And now, I step into a room and remove these clothes because they have more computing power sewn into them than most scientists could house in a university fifteen years ago. They monitor my health. They call an emergency number if I am injured. They inflate if they detect unsafe velocity. All of these devices carry advertisements, messages, they whisper to me, solicit my attention, seduce me into obsession; they shoot invisible arrows into the infoverse that point to me, that determine where I am, that keep an entire office of assistants apprised of my every move. But watch him," Ziechlech points to his number two, "as I remove these clothes and step into that chamber because when I am in that room, I do not exist. I am unseen," Ziechlech unzips his jacket in a fluid swoop. "The relief, I am told, is unimaginable."

Ziechlech steps into the changing pod. He emerges a moment later wearing loose fitting hemp scrubs, looking for all the world like a tired doctor. Before he gets through the inner chamber door, his number two is answering calls and frantically texting. He is reassuring an office of people who had to be kept in the dark about their boss's decision to go dark that the boss is, in fact, in perfect health. The department head places his finger to his ear then stands suddenly more erect. His security detail all shift from being merely attentive to being highly alert. Dogs smelling danger. The federal direct report for regional U.S. business security has called in to find out why Mr. Ziechlech just disappeared.

Inside the chamber, Zen prevails. Ziechlech walks across the slate floor to a redwood bench facing a beautiful garden. Through floor to ceiling glass he sees a fountain, a birdbath, and twenty yards away, bamboo hedges thirty feet tall. A man sits alone playing scrabble on a table at the other end of the room. There is no TV. No overhead. It is perfectly silent.

"Can I join you?" Ziechlech sits at the table. Much of the board is empty. He takes a long look at the old man sitting across from him. The old man stares back.

"Why don't we start over?" The older man swipes all the tiles into a velvet sack. He begins to gently shake the tiles.

"I play a variation," says Z. "We divide all the tiles evenly at the start. No need to hide your letters. It is an open game."

"Practically guarantees a triple word score."

They divide the tiles.

"I am uncomfortable with the not hiding my letters part," Ziechlech tells the man.

They take a few minutes sliding tiles around. Ziechlech leans back and stares at his tiles. The older player does the same.

"I know. I know. Everyone gets upset at first. But with all those letters and combinations lying out in the open like that, well, one must pay very close attention to another's efforts to gain any advantage. And since one is probably spending so much time ordering their own tiles, they really can't afford to pay such close attention to those of their opponent." The older man lazily slides tiles in and out of orders.

"How do I make sense out of this?" Ziechlech pushes a row of adjoined tiles forward.

WHERES DIZZY

"I see your concern," the older man says. "Look at mine." He quickly rearranges tiles.

IDK

"That is very confusing. I don't know if I like this game," Ziechlech quickly reorders his letters.

YOU PROTECT HER

The older man sighs. "I can see why you would arrange them like that but you still haven't got it." He slides tiles:

TAUGHT HER EVERYTHING

Ziechlech puzzles over it. "I find this game alarmingly challenging."

"Yes."

"I must profess, I doubt I am going to enjoy it again."

"Oh, now," the Older man picks up a tile and rolls it through his fingers like a poker chip. "There are great advantages to this game. All the pieces are on the table. You can see what everyone else is doing. There are few unknowns."

"Few?"

"Well, the skill of the players is always unknown until you begin to play. And each player's intentions, their personal vision of possibilities, their dictionary of potential from which they can only choose combinations they are already more or less aware of. No one can create a letter that isn't there, am I right? And then the most distressing query: Are you sitting down with a novice or a master? As soon as they lay their tiles and spell a word," the Older man carefully clicks tiles onto the board:

TRANSITUATIONIST

"Then you know."

"Of course, but a novice," Ziechlech clacks tiles down across the older man's word:

EXPOSED

The older man smiles at the board. He rolls the tile through his fingers. He lays his remaining tiles onto the board then reaches across to Z's pile to steal a few.

ADAPTIVE APPRENTICE

Ziechlech runs his fingers through his hair. The older man stands, smoothes his scrubs.

"It can be an exhausting game when all the possibilities are revealed. Even boring. But for the adaptive apprentice of a master player, each of these tiles represents worlds of possibility—some more than others."

The older man places the tile he has been rolling through his fingers onto the table with a dull snap. He walks out of the room through the portal. He does not retrieve any devices from the clerk.

Ziechlech picks up the tile on the table before him. He rolls it over a couple times and chuckles.

It's blank.

Burning Memories

It all started with a dream. She was in her bed, in her home in Belarus, her family's ancient, gigantic mansion, standing in the conservatory, one wall facing southeast, a perfect sheet of glass two inches thick, reaching from beneath the concrete floor, and disappearing beyond the edge of the ceiling, past the walls on either side, fifty feet wide, not a seam, not a fold, not a crack. If she spoke out loud, she could ask House to lower this wall into the ground then she could step directly into the gardens that lay beyond it to the lake. Her father had told her many times the glass could support the weight of fifty elephants. It can stop a train, he told her.

When she was little, this wall would develop a film of smudge about three feet above the floor as she would walk from one end to the other with her nose sliding along the glass as she watched the landscapers install the gardens. She would go to lunch and return to find the glass perfectly clean.

In her dream [Mary Jennifer Jones] is that child again. She has her nose pressed against the cool glass watching the lake burn. Flames rise sixty feet off the water. The wind whips them toward her. They break and flicker apart into sails of flame tearing away across the grounds like ghosts.

From the middle of the maelstrom a shadow emerges, black, burning, cracking, a skeleton of minarets, balconies, turrets, gaping doors, great carved gates flapping against smoldering stone. This palace stalks toward her gouging a deep trench in the gardens, setting the fig trees aflame. In the windows, through the smoke, she sees princes and princesses, kings and queens, all smiling, all happy, all content; they are going about their business, they are talking quietly, they are telling stories, they are learning to dance.

She yells to House and the wall of glass slithers downward but the heat has expanded the window and it catches halfway—too high for her. She screams. She runs through her father's house. In each room those kings and queens sit sipping tea, their bodies entirely engulfed in fire, oblivious to her screaming. Through the windows she glimpses this pyrotanical palace limping closer, it's foundation rocking as if on stout stubs of legs, the same Kings and Queens smiling from the windows.

There he is, sitting in a chair made of waxed wicker, a massive complicated throne woven from strong bamboo wands. There are limbs within limbs, hidden compartments; tiny caged animals (an eagle, a bull) screech in alarm. Her father beams a smile that shoots through her, warm and radiant, a pearled beam of pure peace. He reaches into the massive, curled arm of his chair, a mesh cabinet; he holds a melon in his hand; he raises his other hand to signal someone across the room, the entire world seems to hang on his request, only wanting to hear his voice, his deep chesty brogue, that mountain that says her name with such absolute and silent power. But her father glances past her and his face sets in concern. [Mary Jennifer Jones] sees his body suddenly shine golden pink. She beats on her father's breast. She pulls him away from the windows but the palace crashes through and [Mary Jennifer Jones] is left alone, watching her father's house burn as she flies backwards away from it all.

[Excerpt from The New Gypsy Tango, Sept. 23, 2025, Wayfarer stream]

You might work with one of them. You might have crowdsourced a new product to them. You might have rented them a floor of your hotel. You may own a hardware store and receive a purchase order for twine, ¼ inch c-hooks, and polypropylene sheeting. You may, like Damien Sanchez, have hired them to streamline your trans Euro hemp exporting business using micro zeppelin drones and technology that maps wind currents on the fly to deliver your bundles a thousand miles, on time, for next to nothing, the way gypsies do.

I don't mean the old painted wagon gypsies (although they still exist!) I mean the new gypsies. The children of remote worker culture. They are wandering techno wizards; wayfaring logistics geniuses; corporations who have not only shed cubicle culture, but the office itself, in fact, the building en toto.

"We go where the work is. We're nomadic," says Wabo James, the public relations liaison for the Api Nomada, an organization of highly skilled professionals who travel and work together as a mobile corporation.

"The common term is *sojourner.* We're not nomadic in the truest sense, since we don't travel in a distinct circuit as traditional nomads," explains Janet Borgan, In House Counsel. "But nomad is close. Look at our title: Api Nomada—the nomadic bees."

Like a corporation, the Api Nomada have a logo, a sign, that distinguishes them from other sojourners (ie: *Caz Ars Noblige,* the House of the Noble Arts, a kind of traveling circus/elementary art program/alchemist's bazaar): a honeybee.

"It comes from old heraldic tradition. A bee was a symbol of industry. Our primary skill is the ability to adopt an existing company and redirect their productivity chain into a more efficient, more profitable, model."

Traveling efficiency experts.

For an idea of how Api Nomada can affect a region, consider their recent work in Barcelona. Api Nomada was brought in to retool their paper industry from wood-sourced to hemp sourced. This was a massive redesign not of a simple industry, but for the economy of the entire region south to Valencia. After Api Nomada was, in their terminology, 'fully extracted', 191,417 new trees had been planted in a carefully randomized pattern that will best mimic original European hardwood forests including 1 million interplantings to ensure undergrowth bio diversity; three new local industries had emerged from the micro business seminars held at the local Api Nomada HQ employing not only ALL the former loggers and logging workers in the region, but all related and subsidiary businesses affected by the change; paper making plants had been retooled or disassembled; printing presses had been retooled or re-calibrated to handle the different resiliencies of hemp paper; new micro businesses had sprung up to create clothing and fabrics from the hemp cloth; failing and subsidized farms were redesigned to grow hemp on a massive scale and at an accelerated initial rate. All of the environmental effects of long-term paper pulping were, in their terms, 'mined' for profitable elimination and removal. Children's grades improved. Asthma cases declined. In fifteen years, Barcelona will be surrounded by healthy hardwood forests populated by indigenous mammals, birds, and insects, groundwater will be clean and no wandering invisible plume of sulfur will drift across the town like a devil of stink.

Most importantly, most remarkably, most incredibly: Api Nomada came in under budget, prior to their deadline, and made a 300% profit on the job due to their accumulation of new patents and technologies which they will share, in perpetuity, with the people of Barcelona.

And that's another interesting difference in how Api Nomada does business. They don't bid for jobs, clients solicit their help in the same way they might solicit a lawyer and it's not the money that seals the job—it's the complexity of the larger picture.

"We don't like being bored. So a job has to offer us a considerable level of complexity or we're gonna pass. And I don't mean it simply has to be difficult. That's a given. I mean the position of the company must be polyvalent, allowing for variegated ingress and egress into related businesses, communities, consumer structures, and economies."

Borgan is quoted elsewhere as saying

[stream terminated]

[Excerpt from "Api Nomada's Mess," May 12, 2055, New Spaniard stream]

Api Nomada may have flipped the nefarious logging industry for an equally nefarious marijuana industry, and perhaps many are quite thrilled, but they left behind a gigantic mess. Will they return to clean the graffiti off our walls? How many of you now have a "2920" scrawled onto the wall of your business? How many plugs have that strange hieroglyphic sticker pasted at eye level so when you're charging, you cannot help but to observe this occult symbol. The number, 2920, stands for BIT, an ancient Egyptian term for 'he of the bee,' as was used to denote royalty, most often a king. The image below is the Egyptian hieroglyph for the same insect. Look familiar? The goddess. You might read it represents industry but how many Barcelonic and regional Spanish businesses feel more like they've been stung?

[EOS]

ECONOMICS

Djara Ziechlech and her father are sitting in a teashop in Chinatown in Chicago. Djara watches the crowd race by. This teashop is shoved into an alcove in the Chinese farmer's market behind a butcher's table on the right and a man selling noodles and legacy office supplies on the left. A steady stream of Chinese run between the blood and boxes of envelopes to get tea. The shop is impossibly noisy and so far, Djara hasn't seen a single person—except for her father—pay for their drink.

"Why don't they pay?"

"Credit."

"But they're not writing anything down."

"They know each other."

"It's so fast."

"Yes."

Her father is noodling on his pad.

"Are you checking the numbers?"

"Playing Scrabble."

"WOT."

"You might think so. But I find it infinitely fascinating. This and logic problems. I can't think of a better way to spend my free time."

"I'd clear my throat meaningfully but I suspect you'd just chuckle and keep looking for a triple word score."

"Not as hard in this game—we're playing extreme Scrabble. See, you divide all the tiles—"

"—evenly among the players and blavum infinitum."

"So bright."

Djara watches the people. She gets into line for another cup. When she gets to the counter, she points at the Oolong, takes her cup, and looks at the proprietor. Djara glances over her shoulder at her table then raises her eyebrows to the man with the ladle in his hands. He juts his chin. She sits.

"Herr Z, I am concerned."

"Yes, my love?"

"You suggested I go on a side-quest yet here I am with no bags, no passport, no nothing. We're sitting in a closet behind a butcher in Chinatown in Chicago. Shouldn't we be at a train station or O'Hare or something more conducive to travel?"

"We're waiting on someone."

"Whom?"

"Your godfather."

"I have a godfather?"

"You do."

"I've never met him."

"Well, not that you can remember," Ziechlech folds up his pad and signals for a cup. An old man in a golf shirt and gray slacks appears almost instantly with a teapot."

"Why haven't I ever met this guy?"

"I've been away," the old man says. He pours tea. He is unremarkable in the most urgent sense of the phrase. His golf shirt could not have cost more than 18 bucks at a public course; his slacks are WalMart grade disposable slampants, breaking deeply over the faces of bright white Nike running shoes. He is either Chinese or Jamaican or Eskimo. He wears no visible tech. One of the tea purveyors, an old woman, is pestering him loudly and the man hasn't even looked at the Ziechlechs. He carries on with the woman, gesturing angrily, his face contorted with frustration, his back three quarters to the table. Djara stares blatantly at this scene, her father seems only mildly interested. As the man gestures to the grandmother and barks curt Chinese, he also speaks to the westerners without looking at them.

"I'm Cable Toje, your godfather," Toje says this while pointing over her head to some hanging junk in the stall. The old woman is screaming an unbroken stream of Mandarin. Toje is speaking in a low, urgent, highly controlled angry voice but none of his words are directed at the crone. "It seems your recent mathematical adventures have alerted the authorities to an anomaly in the investment practices of the businesses your father does business with. In a few hours, your father will receive a call from the fraud division of the American Government's financial policing wing. You have uncovered a horrific scam that will affect trillions of dollars in investments and the livelihood of important people all over the world. You have pointed a finger at evil. Your father will now do that publicly."

Djara is openly staring at Toje. She is also absorbing what he's said. He's right. She knew it as soon as she told her mom. Shit.

Ziechlech leans toward Djara and composes himself as if making a joke about the crazy Chinese arguers. He is smiling, but Djara can see in his eyes it's fake, that he's scared. Suddenly she's terrified.

"Darling, I am always followed, always observed, tracked, recorded, imprinted. In order for me to do anything without this nuisance, I must resort to a little theater. Usually, it's more for fun. Today, you're meeting your godfather because the mistake you found in our accounts is going to ruin many people's livelihoods. I have to proceed cautiously as I reveal this problem so that I don't ruin the lives of many more. All of them are very rich, all of them are powerful. Some of them are dangerous. I will have to work with the government and with America and word will get out and you will be in danger. You *are* in danger," her father laughs at the crazy Chinese.

"So you're going on a little trip with the help of your Godfather; it's all very secret. The security and ambient cameras will record you walking to the loo and then returning."

Toje smacks his forehead and brays at the crone. She returns a fusilade of vociferous cursing.

"Only it won't be you," Toje says. "When the time is right, you will ask the stall woman where the restrooms are. You'll walk through the gap, behind her stall, to a row of portables, and get in line behind some Tibetan monks."

Toje barks loudly at the crone. Their argument becomes Shakespearian. Ziechlech and Djara stare at them. Djara turns to her father with a look of horror. Her father glances at her, she starts to ask him a question, he leans quickly toward her, as if he can't hear over the argument, and, pointing to the tea ladler, speaks into her ear, "Dizzy, I would hold you now. I would press you into my heart and hide you, but I can't. I wish there was another way. More time. But there's not. Now go. Trust Toje's people. I love you. Go!"

Djara stands carefully, confused. Toje backs his hip into the table while yelling at the crone and the bark of the aluminum legs on cement startles Djara to move. She leans into the counter at the front of the line and tries to ask where the loo is at. The people in line complain. The ladler stares at her. The line tells her to go around the side of the stall. The line tells her, sternly, to hurry up.

Djara walks under reams of polystyrene hung between the edge of the tea booth and the rim of the butcher shop. She emerges from the dark short alley into a crowded hallway; everyone's waiting for their turn at a row of portable toilets. One of the lines is comprised almost entirely of Tibetan monks in full regalia, their heads capped in leather slips holding great golden Mohawks. Djara shuffles in place behind a monk. She enters the cramped loo, nose crinkling, to find it occupied by a nearly nude girl who is exactly her height.

"You don't see me."

Djara hardly hesitates, more as if from the heady perfume of the chemical marinade than the shock of realizing every one of the monks walked in and peed with this girl standing right there. But Djara's spent many years being cool, receiving high profile guests at their home on the lake in Belarus and she doesn't ruffle easily.

"Strip."

Djara drops her trousers, rips off her t-shirt, her hoody, her shoes and socks, and stands there underweared. As she takes them off, the girl puts them on. She hands Djara a bag. Inside it is a golden robe, white socks, sandals, and a plume of yellow. And a battery powered razor. Djara looks at the girl.

"Shave, chick. We got no time."

"My hair. . ."

"Will grow back," the girl grabs the razor and looks meaningfully into Djara's eyes. "I was told to say this to you: Dizzy, baby, it's just a thingily ting." Djara's eyes water. It is what her mother used to say to her when she was little and afraid. Her mother who is in Bahrain on business and probably doesn't even know what is going on. Her mother who is smarter than anyone else she's ever met by orders of magnitude. Oh, of course she knows. Of course, these are her instructions, this is her letting Djara— Djara Ziechlech, DZ, Dizzy—know that she should trust. Dizzy grabs the razor and her hair falls into the blue. The girl grabs the razor and drops it into the blue shit. She takes out a lipstick tube and jabs it gently into the middle of Dizzy's forehead. "Welcome to Tibet," she says and pushes Dizzy gently into the crevice between the open hole toilet and the plastic wall. She opens the door to leave and a monk is opening the door to get in. They engage in a close quarters awkward dance, the girl boggling the monk who remains indifferent, just pressing into the lou. Dizzy realizes this is choreographed, that they are blocking cameras. He door slams shut behind the monk. He stares at Dizzy. They're the same height. He takes her hand, pulls her gently from the slot she's shoved into, and pushes her out the door.

Another Monk is waiting for her, bored out of his mind. He walks away without saying a word and Dizzy falls in step. The Monks are all jabbering away. They walk out past the tea stand where Dizzy sees herself join her dad who smiles and stands so they can finish their tour of the market. Dizzy didn't realize how much the girl looks like her. She even stands like her. A monk hands her a plastic shopping bag full of oranges. They exit the farmers market mall into bright sunshine and get onto a tour bus with dark windows. No one talks to her.

The bus jerks and rolls out of Chinatown, onto the Dan Ryan, heads out toward O'Hare. As soon as they're really moving, the monk next to her sighs and removes his head piece. Another mohawkless monk pops up over the tall back of the seat in front of her and sticks his hand through the seat gaps.

"Hey. I'm Freddy and this guy is Zeke," Zeke shakes her hand lightly. All the other monks come by and introduce themselves, and shake her hand, and reassure her that she performed remarkably well at the bathrooms.

"Are you guys, I mean, who hired—"

"We're monks."

"nshit?"

"nshit, baby. Honest to God Tibetan Buddhists. From Omaha."

"Where are we going?"

"Oh, it's convoluted. And we can't tell you," Freddy says.

"Because we don't know. Well, we know where *we're* going, but we have no idea where you'll end up," Zeke informs her. "We don't even know your name."

"I'm-"

"Nope. We don't want to know your name."

"Actually we're giving you a new name."

"Apparently, you're becoming a traveler."

"Is my Dad going to be ok?"

"Oh sure, honey. He's fine. He's already on his way back to the office."

"Look," Freddy and Zeke trade seats. "We're returning a huge favor to Cable Toje. He asked us to escort you onto our tour plane, take you to our next stop, and deliver you into the waiting arms of some friends you've never met."

"What kind of favor?"

"A big favor. We hired his company to help us settle in Nebraska and they did such an amazing job, well, we feel pretty obligated to help him out any way he wants pretty much any time he needs us."

A voice comes over the intercom.

"Zeke, play the file."

"On it," Zeke unfurls a scroll. Toje is smiling, drinking tea in the stall with the Chinese crone, who is all smiles. The picture is jerky and handheld.

"Djara, these men are going to fly you to Orlando. I know this is weird and I know you're freaking out right now, but this subterfuge is vital to your safety. The Monks are going to take you with them to Orlando where you will all be tourists. At some point, you will meet someone who will be calling to you using a new name. I don't know what that name is. Neither does your dad. It's all secret double-oh-seven rigamarole."

He sips his tea. The Chinese woman says something to Cable, her voice is syrupy and kind.

"Right. You're disappearing dizzy. Everything that happens to you from this point will involve less and less technology until you reach a point where it might as well be 1983. We're essentially wiping you off the grid to hide you from some very bad people whom your father is about to stop doing business with. It's going to be weird and ... Dizzy. In order to make you truly untouchable, we have to make parts of the adventure real."

The Chinese woman smacks Toje in the shoulder and admonishes him in warm Chinese.

"Right. Look, Dizzy, no matter how weird this gets, don't be scared. It's an adventure. So, Enjoy the monks, they're not what most people expect." The file ends. The monk holding the plastic box that played the file throws it out the window vent onto the highway.

"Yeah, we skate."

"So what's my name?"

One of the monks hands her a piece of rolled up paper. She unfolds it into a tiny square.

Jennifer Maria Jones.

The monks have gone quiet. One of them grabs the paper from her, tosses it out the vent where the wind snatches it and it disappears.

"Don't tell us. Don't tell anyone."

"And if anyone calls you by your real name?"

Dizzy looks up at the faces crowded over the back of the seat.

"Run."

Dizzy puts her forehead against the glass and cries quietly as Chicago's rooftops flash behind her. The El passes by, revealing the back of a graffiti crusted billboard where someone has painted a giant white square and inside of it, a stylized bee.

PARLAY

Tosh bounds through the trailer early in the morning, singing, making tea, loading his pipe. [Mary Jennifer Jones] extracts herself from her hammock in her room and shuffles fore into the galley. Tosh is wearing a captain's hat over his stubby dreads.

"Permission to board," [Mary Jennifer Jones] holds out her cracked teacup. It's decorated with examples of nautical knots.

"Permission granted, stowaway." Tosh pours deep brown tea from one bent copper tumbler into another, playing the stream out wide and foaming the whole mess like a Mumbai tea walla.

"Not that you aren't usually a fountain of joy, but why so happy today, Captain?"

"We're coming along the mail drop."

"Seriously? Mail? Like letters?"

"And parcels, and bundles, postcards, bulls, B2B, Christmas cards—"

"Bat Mitzvah cards."

"Bills."

"Duns"

"Summonses."

"Edicts."

"Notices to appear."

"Why are yours trending toward legal and mine trending toward royalty?"

"It only comes once a week now."

"Isn't it ridiculously dear?"

"Yes. What, two bucks for a postcard?"

"Mostly a tourist anachronism."

"But"

"Ah, this is why I like you, fugitive, you always shoot for the heart of it, for the motivation. You are an investigator."

"I am not."

"You are. You cannot stand not to know the origin of something, the etymology. You're an etymologist of the meaning of everything."

"But. . ."

"I am not a hermit. I do enjoy my peripheral life. But even I have friends and as the ship sails around the world, it periodically comes to mail drops and I get to hear from the distantly marooned. Today, I have received a missive from *royalty*." Tosh's face tints with anticipation. He's giddy. He sweeps his arm toward the table where a twine-wrapped box acts as base for a stack of postcards and letters. On top, like a groom on a cake, is a beautiful invitation. [Jennifer Jones] picks it up. Tosh sips tea and watches her with blatant regard, eating it up.

The invitation is complicated. Jewelish. A cream colored envelope wrapped with a black ribbon and sealed with a deep crimson wax blob the size of a half dollar. The raised image in the wax knob is a ship with sails pregnant in the wind, rising up against a wave, the main sail imprinted with an ornate MC. It is addressed to Capt. Peter Aurelius Tosh of the Octavius.

Tosh gestures his mug toward the envelope. "Go ahead."

[Jones] takes her time. She peels the seal off the paper with little damage. She slips the envelope open and removes a thick card. The paper is bamboo parchment with vertical stripes of slightly darker white and dead center, written in a delicious calligraphy, are the following words:

> *The Mary Celeste shall moor*
> *for the feast of St. Jean the Baptiste*
> *on the island of A A Hippo*
> *in the body of the Russian's daughter.*
> *You are encouraged to bring*
> *a friend.*

[Jones] reads it out loud.

"Well, at least he's not at all cryptic."

"A habit of sailors."

"That sounds like a euphemism."

Tosh pours more tea. "He's also a sea captain."

"Oh my god. You guys are like cosplay freaks but for boats."

"Ships."

"Oh here we go. Is the Mary Celeste really a ship? And why would he spend so much time and effort making this beautiful invite but then leave such a glaring grammatical error and one he made in slomo penwork?"

Tosh reads the card.

"No mistakes."

"A *a* hippo? I think just *a* hippo would suffice, or le hippopotamus, or un reever peeg."

"Hmm."

Tosh smiles at the invite then smiles at [Jones].

"The island of the hippos is some secret meeting place isn't it?"

"You could say that. And more interestingly, you've been invited."

"How?"

"The Mary Celeste gets around."

"Are we going to sail? That's trick!"

"Oh, no, stowaway. The Mary Celeste is not a ship. The Mary Celeste is a *man*. And the feast of St. John the Baptiste is the summer solstice and the island of A A Hippo is the city of Aurelius Augustinus Hipponensis. The friend, however, would be *you,* stowaway and how the Mary Celeste knew I had a friend in stowage is beyond even my powers of deduction. The guy knows a lot of people."

"Who's the Russian's daughter?"

"Well, I can't tell you everything, can I? Enough to say we're taking an adventure. Pack your shit, such as it is; we shove off this afternoon."

"Where the hell are we go—hey, I kind of need to sick around."

"Don't worry, castaway, you travel in my protection. Under the radar. We're going to the port of St. Augustine. We'll eat crab claws and drink

Hurricanes. We'll parlay with the Mary Celeste and get drunk on Nelson's Folly."

"Oh my god, you're not pretending to be *captains,* you're pretending to be *pirates!*"

"Aye, castaway, ye be on the money."

Poker Face

"I don't understand."

Cable Toje had a tell. Everyone who worked for him knew it. He knew it. He managed to stay out of high stakes single hand poker[1] but in regular conversation, when he's working, if things get hairy, he rubs his fingers together like he's counting money. In fact, he probably is counting something; could be anything: the number of people in the room wearing tennis shoes, iterations of the name "Frank" in outsourced Indian dock workers, or the creases in his potential client's cromagnificent forehead, an edifice currently prohibiting his potential client from comprehending how he and his fellows of the Nash Equilibrium armada might save the man millions of dollars sure to be wasted on maintenance of this medieval buttress poorly camouflaged by warring caterpillar eyebrows.

What Toje wants to explain to his caveman friend: that by applying complex gaming models to logistics and efficiency systems to the man's growing business, millions of dollars will be saved over the next ten years. It is money that would otherwise disappear into wasted efforts, fuel costs, downtime, and all kinds of fines, refunds, and shrink. All he has to do is turn his team loose—Well, they're not a team yet. But his current armada, the Api Nomada, is becoming cumbersome and the core managers have determined that it's time to split a chunk off into a new independent fleet which they'll turn around and immediately hire. But Toje wants to run some customers through first, some small shit, so the fleet can develop a sense of camaraderie and joi d vivres which he feels ought to embody the spirit of their namesake, the Nash Equilibrium, a game theorem Toje always saw as a metaphor for a game that's the most fun to play because it ensures mutual success for all players. Or mutual doom. (But for doom you'd have to have a bunch of gamers whose personal strategy was negative, which he does not.) The NE is comprised of top-level polygamers from a couple of Armadas, primarily the AN, in which he remains an elder partner. They're itching for proof and this guy's business is a logistical tragedy.

"Ok, so you're telling me I would pay you seventy million dollars—

---

1 Though he remained the reigning champion at three-handed Texas hold'em, also called "3 Rivers Poker" in which three iterations of Texas hold 'em are played simultaneously. There are three flops, three turns, and three rivers (hence the name). Players can apply any combination of the turns, flops, and rivers onto their three hands, but must stick with their combination once they've bet. 123 chips are set onto the flops and each player sets their own 123 chip onto which hand they intend to play that combo onto. Combos can be changed any time during play until the deal is sealed before the rivers.

seventy MILLION dollars—"

"Over four years."

"—to play games?"

"Mr. Hannity, what we do is apply high level mathematical models to your business environment to pursue and capture increasingly more efficient and successful moves for your company, resulting in increasingly greater rewards."

"I already have number crunchers, Mr. Tow, I have a whole floor of them."

"But they're accountants. They're looking exclusively at accounts payable and receivable. We look at everything. We look at the brand names on your paper supplier's delivery trucks. We look at your customers' books. We look at your uniform suppliers. We look at the weather."

"You sound like wizards."

"Math wizards. Sure. Look, give us a month at 60 on the dollar. If we don't tune your numbers by 50%, you don't pay us a dime. And we guarantee a minimum 10% increase in your gross so even if you don't pay us, you come out ahead. You've got nothing to lose."

Toje takes a jet back to Vegas where he's been scouting with two other Api EPs. They come over Nevada an hour after sunset. Toje's riding in the cockpit with his feet up on the dash and a Negroni in his hand. The pilot's jacked in to an ambient list wearing flight goggles in his seat in the middle of the plane, the whole thing like a holographic hallucination in which he is the plane and he's in a movie about flying. Toje's all by himself when Vegas tips over the black horizon like an overblown Christmas ornament. The airport's ten miles outside the city but they skirt the rim of the joint and he watches it slide under him.

He remembers back when he was a boy and his parents took him to Disney for the first time and he rode Peter Pan's Adventure. The ride managers called the cartooned cars gondolas and he got in between his moms and the bar squeezed them all in and they shot up into the sudden night sky. He remembers rounding a bend that was black invisible and finding himself over a miniature London, circa 1915. For a moment, he saw the whole thing for what it was, a fiberglass board with tiny lamp lights running on tracks to simulate cars and houses and then it was gone and he was floating over London and he marveled.

Now he floats over the real Las Vegas. It slides underneath him exactly like he's hanging in a gondola in an air-conditioned warehouse of a ride in Florida in 1998 and his ribcage longs for the press of his moms against him. But they are far away, flung like debris from a bomb, one landing in Oviedo, FL, working for NASA; one gouging a trail into the flatlands of Illinois, a meteor of fire and thunder, burying herself in a trench of crystal meth and bad girlfriends before coming to a sudden stop against the side of a church.

The plane drops down to skim over the Simulate Sea, installed and maintained by the original Armada, the [xxx], all gone, all dispersed into the current travelers, like the twelve tribes of Israel, circling the world.

They land so perfectly he's not even sure it happened. He just looks up from his drink and notices the tarmac isn't moving.

There's a turquoise 1966 Chevy Impala drop-top parked next to the plane with its engine running. Toje gets in and drives away.

Vegas is a nightmare. It rolls over him, a tunnel of light, a cocoon of LEDs and plasma. The sun is long gone but everyone wears shades. Everything is deeply glossed, reflective, lacquered, diamond. Toje tells his car to drive randomly. He ignores the highway, reaches into his valise, pulls out his scroll and a couple of Skull pops. He balances his drink on the console and stretches his legs out across the front seat. He absent mindedly reaches out and mutes the screen. There's more than enough light. His scroll unrolls transparent green. He calls up the Nash Equilibrium tree and begins tracking scores.

ANOMALY

Mrs. Ziechlech has a thing for Prague, historic Russian princesses, and cartography. Djara climbs to the top of the stairs in a classic teen mope. She's wearing flesh-colored layered crinoline and a poufy net dress, emerald dreadlocks, bright crimson army boots, and bronze steampunk goggles capable of displaying an inset video of various eyes, including 'night eyes-lion' and 'lorax,' shoved up to the widow's peak of her cyberpunk wig. Djara's carrying heavy news.

She leans her forehead against the green marble wall lining the hallway at the top of the stairs, looks out the far windows through the garden to the lake where afternoon sun sparkles and a tiny helium skier swings past. She rolls her back onto the marble and it gives, a solid rectangular slab falling away on invisible hinges.

Djara loves her mother's library, the dark woods, the cartographic walls cycling through 400 years of beautiful maps, the brass. She drags her fingers along the spines of trade paperbacks; along glass cabinets vacuum sealed and climate controlled housing actual scrolls that would crumble in the still breath of the room; along the knobbly ridges of old leather captain's logs. She can see the great globe of her mother's office looming into view through the passage at the end of the library. She can see her mother.

The wall behind her is an aerial video of an energy rig off the coast of Argentina where the wind turbines were torn off in a sudden squall. Smaller windows show the sub cams, the rig foot cams, and a room of worried people, some on screens, all looking into a table. One of the men turns to the room.

"Z, there's just no way to catch it. You know the currents."

"I do know the currents, Mitchell, which is why you will drop a catch exactly where I've marked and we will snag your turbine before it crashes through that ridiculous hotel."

The man looks past Mrs. Ziechlech. "Hi, Dizzy."

Mrs. Z turns. Djara waves to the engineer who waves back. He sees this whip thin cyber princess with the sunlight from her mother's office wall streaming through her skirts, her body and face really a dark brown blur, but her stance, the universal teenage tilt, the hands cupping the elbows, the stare. He looks at his boss. "I'm gonna conserve. We'll get back to you," and his window disappears.

"I've discovered an anomaly."

Djara says this tentatively, she says this as her fingers dip into the globe and it snaps to, showing real time clouds where her finger hangs over the north Atlantic. Mrs. Z whispers 'default' and all the windows on her wall disappear, the walls themselves reverting back to her collection of maps, faded to barely visible, a burnished gold all around the room. The sun shines a shadow on the wall from the globe, an eclipse in miniature.

"In your lessons?"

"Yep."

"You tested it against the templates we provided?"

"Yep."

"What kind of anomaly?"

"It's a transactional bulge I couldn't verify so I ran some math and it looks as if the streams entering do not match perfectly with the streams recorded. Further math revealed a stream that followed a tangential association with an account region that piled it into another region where it all seems to end up . . . there's a lot of money skipping our records. Someone's bypassing us and putting a lot of money somewhere else."

"Djara, that's impossible. The only reason we're in business is because we're quad redundant. Our records are purposefully transparent and—you must've done something wrong." Mrs. Z calls up the lesson Djara worked on. The lesson is their business model and Djara is learning quality control of multithreaded tertiary income streams from multithreaded micro investment models that converge in a bank model from their very dear friend, Sub Cartesian Blankenship, which the Ziechlech's then record and, based on their recordings—and this part is vital to their business—report to the various tax models associated with the upstreams and the income model of each client. The Z's distribute reports quarterly and the clients base their taxes entirely on the Z's report. It's thoroughly scanned by various networks, reported on annually, and can affect the economies as much as Wall Street on any given day. A glitch is bad. An anomaly would be catastrophic.

Mrs. Z studies the scroll on her desk. She drops her forehead down into her hands. She shoves her fingers into her hair. She closes her eyes. She opens them again, sea foam green glossy eyes wrecked with fear. She curls her hands over her mouth. She looks over her fingers at Djara.

"Oh my God, Dizzy. Oh my God. We're ruined."

THE GRAVITY HARP

Tosh and [Mary Jennifer Jones] head north to St Augustine, a gorgeous sun blown rock of a city, but it feels like they will never get there. I-4 Northeast is a slow majestic imminently safe procession of autcars and blind busminivans and then there is a long county road, a perfectly straight line bordered by pine hammocks and bait shops. The Mormons bought all the land along this half-highway in the punk decade for reasons no one really understands nor wants to look into. Only wild animals and redneck fishermen have managed to wedge themselves deeper than twenty feet into the tangle just off the highway in the last 45 years. The trees are bearded and shot through with lantana and wild asparagus. The truck is a piece of crap, gas only, no navtech, no radio, no air conditioning.

Tosh loves it. He sings loud into the wind while [Jones] lays her head on her arm in the sun in the open window and stares into the green blur of the shoulder.

Tosh drives like an old man in the unhurried determined passage of the permanently stoned. He's got a warm sopping bag of boiled peanuts in the cup holder, a delicacy [Mary Jennifer Jones] rejects with unabashed, nauseated disdain. She's got road food rules. Her fingers absently dip into a bag of hot buttered flash roasted nanotots pulled out of a vending machine at a biker bar just past Daytona.

When St. Augustine finally shows up, it does it in jagged reveals: a barrier of t-shirt shops and coffin motels, then a second tier of high-end chain restaurants and charging stations, then an elegantly appointed ring of expensive hotels and name dropper restaurants. Finally they pass over a bridge through a corridor of truly enormous live oaks and magnolias trailing Spanish moss like a fog and the old city leaps out at them, ancient sister of New Orleans, buildings old as dirt, refinished, retooled, repainted in a contemporary version of a elder style but still Spanish, still Jesus old. They pull into the lot at the fort and take the tour. The docent is dressed like a Spanish conquistador with a chrome helmet and slit velvet pantaloons but he's not sweating a drop and [Mary Jennifer Jones] leans in close to hear the whir of tiny little turbines sewn inside the costume running a thin film of cool air under the fabric.

They stoop to walk into the dungeon. [Mary Jennifer Jones] wonders at the ancient graffiti: the styles, the language. They pick a spot along the eastern wall and watch dolphins shoot through the bay. Tosh pulls out a flask and offers a toast to the ocean. They nip explosive shots of homemade rum. They leave. They tool around the city, past the tiny useless planetarium, ringed and shadowed by trees. They make a plan to visit the fountain of life, the old Ringling Museum, an ancient bar. Finally they drive south out of the city, cross a bridge, and find themselves on Anastasia Island.

"The Russian's Daughter," [Jones] notes.

There, under an oak with branches thick as tree trunks resting on weathered cement support pylons, is a contraption. [Mary Jennifer Jones] can't take her eyes off it. Like a brilliant mash-up of a wicker patio set and a 19th century horse-drawn hearse and a frigate and a gypsy wagon. There's a goat tied off the back-end munching grass. There's a chicken too. Swinging in a hammock chair is a late middle-aged man with a magnificent beard. He's smoking a pipe as big as a coffee cup and tending a little complicated stove. As he catches Tosh's eye, he drops slowly out of his hammock chair, lithe and graceful, and walks to the edge of his camp. Tosh meets him there with [Jones].

"Permission to come aboard the Mary Celeste?"

"Permission granted, Capt. Tosh."

They stand still for a split second then grab each other in an enthusiastic bear hug and slaps on the back and how you doin's and offers of drink and smoke and finally Tosh turns to [Jones].

"Captain Butler, [Mary Jennifer Jones], [Mary Jennifer Jones], William Yeats Butler, Captain of the Mary Celeste."

They settle onto camp chairs. Butler pours lemonade. He runs a wedge around the rim of a glass, dips it into sugar, fills the tumbler with cracked ice, then pours lemonade from a giant handblown glass pitcher, huge hunks of lemon floating in it like snowflakes, a slice on the rim as a garnish. He folds a Murphy table down from the back of his wagon, tosses a gorgeous white cloth over it, and sets a snack of cucumbers, strawberries, sliced mango, papaya, and goat cheese with pepper flakes. Tosh gets his boiled peanuts out of the truck.

"What brings you to St. Augustine, Capt. Butler?"

"I'm here to tune their Gravity Harp."

[Mary Jennifer Jones] does a spit take. "Gravity Harp?"

"Here in the botanical gardens, I installed it fifteen years ago. A worthy commission."

"Is it heavy?" [Mary Jennifer Jones] sips her lemonade carefully.

"Sixteen tons or so."

"Tee eff."

"It's mostly granite and brass, with some copper pipes and wax and dirt. It's quite cathedral."

"I got to see this."

They pack up. Butler opens a closet on the side of the Merry Celeste and he and Tosh wrestle a couple of folding bikes to the ground. Butler yanks a giant hoop off the other side. It is merely a wheel with two pedals and no cranks at all. The rim is a tightly woven shell, highly shellacked. Butler steps inside his wheel, kicks a pad back and shoots forward. [Mary Jennifer Jones] can't stop laughing. Their foldy bikes are half recumbent half Big Wheel. They fall in behind Butler. [Mary Jennifer Jones] laughs all the way through the botanical gardens as workers and afternoon strollers stop and stare at Butler's hoop, clapping their hands and laughing. They round a stand of giant elephant ears and come to an open circle of green.

In the center, a ring of seven granite pillars rises out of a circle paved with large, flat river rocks. There are holes in the paving, holes the size of a quarter, holes the size of a dime. Children are running all over, covering the holes with their feet and shouting at each other to be quiet. They stop as the bikes show up then surround Butler's wheel. He hands it off to one of the kids who zooms away toward a great fountain, all the kids running after him, screaming.

They all stand there looking at the granite pillars. Butler leaps on top of the shortest one, more like a table, and puts his hands on his hips, closes his eyes, and cocks his head. He stands perfectly still. Suddenly, [Mary Jennifer Jones] realizes the pillar is sinking very slowly. Then she hears a low moan coming from a hole, then another moan from another hole, then a low whistle. She oh my gods and runs around covering holes to change the tones. Tosh climbs up onto another pillar, which she has not noticed is rising at the same tempo Butler's is sinking and all the tones change. New holes moan and whistle. [Mary Jennifer Jones] looks around at the seven obelisks. They are sunk into perfectly fitted shafts. She looks at Butler and a grin practically splits her head in two. She leaps up beside him then takes the harp in great bounds. The children scream back into the circle fighting for turns on the Wheel and a handful break off to join [Jones] on her pillar since she weighs more than them and maybe they can get some real sound. And it works. Air wails out of several holes. Butler and Tosh leap to the highest pillar and [Jones] and her kids join them, all embracing and pressing against each other in unabashed scream laughing as the pillar sinks beneath them and the holes blow a fugue of dried leaves and dust into the air. A couple of parents take a perch and soon the harp is playing, pillars rising and falling, the holes singing a Goreckian movement punctuated with urgent, joyful instructions, screams, and giggling.

Butler looks at [Jones] and a chord of thrill, a recognition of vision, fastens itself between them and tightens. She stands, panting, puts her hands on her hips and shouts.

"Ahoy!"

"Aye, stowaway."

"I think I like the cut of your jib, Capt."

Butler grins at her. He adopts the pose of an orator.

"We sail a sea of light searching for islands of joy."

[Mary Jennifer Jones] stares for a minute at the captain, then over at Tosh who is on the pavers with his hands and feet covering holes while some kid is perched on his arched back. His parents take a picture.

[Jones's] body fills suddenly, as if there were a wind inside her, and she throws back her head and sings loudly into the blue sky.

"Yo ho ho, it's a pirate's life for me!"

Everyone joins in.

Butler sits on the edge of his pillar, now the highest of them all, his naked feet dangling nine feet off the ground. He drums the granite and observes [Jones].

The kids eventually return to Butler's wheel and after scrawling notes into a brown board notebook, Butler steps into his wheel and leads them all through the gardens, back to the Mary Celeste. They pile into Tosh's truck and head over to Butler's preferred roost, the Oxford English Dictionary.

They push the heavy glass doors open into a world of paper, words, and wood. The first thing [Jones] notices is there's no music. The next thing she notices are the walls—floor to ceiling bookshelves loaded with books, old type trays, printer's blocks, inkwells, and pens. The next thing she notices are the taps, easily 30 of them, each promising an amber of peculiar quality, born from a single vat, hovered and fussed over by a bearded chap in a shirt labelled "Alechemist". Butler heads for a sitting room at the back and even though the bar is full, no one is in the leather wingbacks. He settles into the chair, props a pince nez onto the arch of his nose and goes over his notes. An Alechemist comes over with three frosty glasses of a deep dark golden beer. The words "Final Draft" are etched over a logo of an open book.

People everywhere are reading, taking notes. Conversations are quiet, hushed. There are no screens.

The booth nearest them empties. [Jones] walks over to look at the set-up. Against the wall, the bookshelves sport a small framed photograph and a brass plaque, "Michael Ondaatje" and a collection of first editions. There's a box; where most bars would present napkins, salt & pepper, the OED serves blank paper, sharpened pencils, highlighters, post-its, and an eraser.

She goes back to her great bat-winged chair. There's a small table holding her beer on a stack of engineering spec books and a menu. She looks it over, all the entries exactly like a page in a dictionary. She orders *Pigeon a'la Price,* a squab cooked in a ceramic shell, served with a jeweler's hammer, and nanotots with truffle oil. The Bicycle King orders edamame. Tosh gets a B52, a donculous beef sandwich with gravy fries. They wallow in luxury. They tour the bar. They play eucher. The King fake reads her hand as tarot cards, proclaiming she'll develop an obsession with clown tattoos and marry a loud real estate tycoon named Steve. They get another beer, a bright pilsner, "First Draft," and finally a bourbon barrel aged bourbon stout, "Manuscript," as black as ink. [Jones] is digging the day's afterglow, the firefly light of a long wonderful day. She's 17, drunk and stoned, her body champagned from laughing since daybreak.

"So, [Jones]," Butler says after shuffling cards for a prolapsed stoney moment. "What do you do?"

"'m good at math."

"I assumed. But that's a skill, not an occupation."

"I don't have an occupation."

"How about an avocation?"

"Our stowaway is currently a stowaway," Tosh explains.

"I've been told."

"What were you told?" [Jones] is suddenly alert.

"I was told not to tell."

"You can tell me," [Jones] says over the top of her stout.

"Captains' code prohibits parlay, I'm afraid."

"Oh, dear," Tosh says. "Serious."

"It is quite serious."

"Alright, Captain, spill it."

"Well, Ms. [Jones], I was informed that you've had your lessons interrupted and are in need of an instructor. I have agreed to fulfill that role."

"You're a teacher?"

"Yes."

"Who informed you? How did—*Why* did someone inform you?"

"A mapmaker."

[Jones'] mind reels in a memory of her mother's office, the ornate cartography, the nautical embellishment—her very occupation. Suddenly, [Jones] can't speak.

Butler stands and takes [Jones] by the hand.

"I know you've been traveling a lot and then holed up with Capt. Tosh. You've taken a false identity and relinquished all traceable tech. You've had to castle. But it's all been a purposeful road. A living road. To bring you here, to me." He pauses in the hallway leading from the bar back to the garden. In a lighted case nestled into the wall is a scale model of the *Pride of Baltimore*, perfectly detailed, except for three tiny fingerprints along the stern. In the next case, a scale model of the *Mary Celeste* stacked over a model of the *Oerilius* and hanging over them all, a map of Brest Harbor from 1986, and another model, a luxury yacht, *The Gillespie*.

[Jones] is too drunk, too high, to get choked up but she's still too choked up to talk. She just looks up at Tosh.

"You know these vessels?"

She nods.

"You know this map maker?"

She nods. She indicates the last model and croaks, "Not this one."

Butler smiles.

"Aye, ye know her. Ye know her galley fore and aft. It's the *Gillsepie*, named for the jazz trumpeter. You know—"

She looks up.

"Dizzy. Dizzy Gillespie."

Her eyes widen.

"Dizzy," Butler says her name with such affection, such warmth. A tear creeps out of her eye and peeks over her lashes. Tosh takes her hand gently.

"These ships—" Tosh points to them in turn, "are us. That's your father, that's Butler, I'm the *Oerillius*. These ships and a very, very few not displayed here, form a fleet." He squeezes her hand and looks down at her with a face that could hold back a platoon, a face that melts a little when he says "A family."

Butler stares at the ships. Crosses his arms.
"An Armada."

HIBISCUS

"Economics"

She is 12 and flying into Veranassi. Her father holds her hand walking down the steps to the runway where a dented, rusty, beaded, torquoise busminivan flings loud jangly hindipop into the air. Djara is used to limos smooth as granite slabs but she plays it cool, getting into the rickety, reeking busminivan.

They bounce down the middle of the road through a maelstrom of segways and scooters, an otherwise soundless conversation of beeps and curses, excuse mees and no worries, no worries.

The busminivan lurches into a market stall. They pile out and Djara discovers she's at the flower market. Everywhere, billions of cut flowers: a man in a blue sarong with a blue dot in the middle of his forehead sews yellow dandelion heads onto a thread that coils at his feet. There must be a hundred pounds of flowers roped around his shins. Her father hands the man a crumpled note and the man lays several strands of flowers around their necks.

They walk towards a gate on the other side of the market, passing some men wearing long robes of flat flowers; past a crowded fort of 5 gallon buckets filled with flower blossoms surrounding a boy and his mother. The boy takes money and shouts orders and the mother flails around pulling flowers from the buckets, piercing them onto a stick, dipping them into a sweet batter then quickly deep frying them in a roiling metal cauldron of ghee. There are racks of prefried sticks with the same sugared flowers, the boy bundling them and handing them out. There's no line, no order, just a knot of people shouting at the boy, the boy shouting at his mother, the mother shouting back to the boy, and the boy shouting back at the people. Ziechlech steps into the mob around the stand and they melt away. He picks up two sticks of fried hibiscus, the boy snatches a bill out of his fingers and never even looks at him, just keeps shouting. Djara looks at her dad as he hands her the flowers then shoves an entire stick into his mouth, pulls it out clean, closes his eyes and mmmms. She delicately bites through a petal, looks at the cross section of the pastry, the bright pink labellum cradled in the hot sticky sugar dusted crust. It tastes like a rose flavored donut. She devours the rest.

They pass through a sky-blue arch into the weavers bizarre. Her father stops to take it in. Looms are everywhere weaving impossible webs of yarn, every color, every grade.

Djara watches a nappy strand of ochre twine itself around an ancient pillar, an old woman crouched in the gloom, running a spinner with her feet, jabbering away into a skullbud.

"See," her father reaches into a big garbage can of silk worm pods and rills them through his fingers as the old woman redirects her stream of jabber into a trill of cursing at her father's rudeness. He pads his hands together and bows toward her, excusing himself into the background.

"It begins with nature," he takes her hand and they follow the process around the bizarre as silk and wool and hemp become thread and twine and yarn.

Ziechlech kicks a huge spindle of blue yarn. "Still, after all that work, it's nothing but another resource. Useless. Until," he points to a skirt maker who flops reams of new hemp bolt onto a board. The man deftly slices pieces which he flings into a tub on his left. After a flurry of slicing and tossing, he shoves the tub over to a woman seated in a crouch who runs the pieces through a terrifying, menacing, antique sewing machine powered by her feet constantly rocking a board. In a flash, she snaps a finished skirt out of the maw of the machine like a sail catching the wind. Djara turns there in the center of a massive vibrant web of millions of threads all coming to this point.

"It all converges to become cloth. Better than thread but still, a resource. But these people give that cloth structure. Purpose. Meaning. Suddenly all this stuff becomes a skirt, clothing. Suddenly it's useful. These skirts are joined by jackets, blouses, cuffs, socks, slippers, all of it becoming a wardrobe, all of it repeated a billion times around the world."

He touches his fingers to his mouth then makes a peace sign and almost instantly a tea walla is serving them chai, streaming a steaming brown thread from one plastic pot to another, building a perfect froth. Djara can't help but to see how this is his way of making it more useful.

"Our business, Dizzy, collects all these threads and gives them structure. Only, of course, it's not yarns but streams of worth and it isn't skirts, it's a far more complicated wardrobe."

Memory Palace

"How do you know how to put it together?" Dizzy is sitting in a chair in her father's office in their house on the shores of Lake Naroch. It's winter and cold as hell. The lake is a solid sheet of impenetrable ice. You could park a skyscraper on it. Her father is engaging in his winter past-time: building a remote controlled model sailing ship, a reproduction in miniature of his favorite, the Pride of Baltimore, now a tourist ship from Maryland that he visited as boy. His model is a kit designed by a Brest native, a retired ship builder whose grandfather helped build the Pride II after the original sank in 1986. This model is actually the Chausser, a pirate ship often called the Pride of Baltimore, captained by the legendary American privateer, Thomas Boyle.

"It's a pirate ship, sweetheart. So I can put it together any way I want to."

"Are those instructions?" Dizzy hops down from her chair and bounces over to the table where a six-foot long cardboard box holds a jumble of spires and twine and brass. Dizzy picks up a brass lantern the size of a raspberry, steals her fathers cup of tea, and glances at the great map of the ship, unfolded before him on another table. She goes back to her seat and sips the warm drink. "They won't work."

Ziechlech is slowly removing carefully wrapped boxes of scale decking from the bigger box and looking at each one, marveling at the detail. Each plank is a perfect reproduction of actual marine timbers, made from the original blueprints recovered from a Boston dig. He turns the long delicate plank in his fingers, like a stiff linguine. He turns back to Dizzy.

"What do you mean? Of course it will work."

"You're missing B-18, the *capelage de haubans et de l'etai sur le ton de mat.*"

"The what?"

"Page 7."

Ziechlech looks over at the plans rolled out onto the blueprint table. They're 4 up and on page 7 he sees an insert illustration for rigging the mains'l labeled B and part 18 is a top mast rig for securing the sail. Ziechlech carefully works through the box but cannot find a clear Ziploc bag labeled B-18.

The box is a picture of complex order. The Brestian modeler, Syichvia, is well known for his detail, for his presentation, and for knowing just how much work to do so that he presents a complete kit but still allows the builder to consider the boat hand crafted. He packs his own boxes, packing each part in cotton in a Ziploc bag which he inflates like a little balloon before packing it into its row of other neatly packed, slightly inflated Ziploc bags. Each one has a mailing label with the part number stuck neatly in the upper rightmost edge, just under the zipper. His box moves from B-17 to B-20. Two parts missing.

"There are two missing pieces, D—"

"Nope. B19 is in the wrong place."

"Show me!"

"Bottom right, between S-31 and 32."

Ziechlech's eyes dart to the coordinates and there is B-19, in the wrong place, exactly where Dizzy said. Ziechlech replaces it in its proper spot.

"Dizzy, would you like more tea?"

Dizzy looks over the rim of the cup with guilty enthusiasm.

"Sorry, Daddy, I took your tea."

"You're not usually allowed."

"I know. But it's *so good!*"

"Come."

They go into the kitchen, into the glass-fronted pantry. Neatly labeled shelves line the walls, an apothecary cabinet sealing the end of the pantry like a complicated door. Dizzy walks behind her father as he edges into the narrow closet. She's humming a song. He opens a drawer on the apothecarian. He fills a mesh strainer with loose tea from the drawer. They walk out. The trip from the office to the pantry and out could not have taken more than three minutes, including selecting a big fat blue cup from the cup tree on the counter for Dizzy.

Ziechlech places the ball of a strainer into the cup, fills it with boiling water from an instant tap, then places the cup on a flat black coaster. As the tea steeps, the coaster displays a dim blue circle around its base counting down from three minutes.

Ziechlech opens the fridge for cream. He opens a cabinet for sugar. The coaster makes a tiny bell sound. Ziechlech pours in the cream, stirs in the sugar. He hands the massive cup to Dizzy. She holds it with both hands, more like a bowl than a cup.

"Dizzy, which book is missing from the dictionary in the hallway?"

"Number 23."

"How many people are on the lake outside our kitchen?"

"Mr. Kriek is sailing that little ice dingy again. There's a blue snowmobile, another blue—there's seven."

"And in the tea cabinet, which tea is fourth down and seventh over?"

"Oolong raspberry cream."

Ziechlech pulls the silverware drawer out of its slot under the counter. He dumps it onto the floor causing Dizzy to spill her tea a little.

"How many?"

She can't see from her stool on the other side of the counter.

"12 knives, 12 forks, 11 spoons."

Ziechlech looks at the pile of silver on the floor. His wife, Madison, comes in with her hands in her hair. She's wearing a headset.

"It was Daddy!"

"What the hell, Zee?"

"How many?"

"What the hell! Why did you—Dizzy?"

"How many of each?"

"It's a service for twelve."

"Dizzy?" Her father looks straight at his wife.

"I told you already."

"Diz."

"12 forks, 12 knives, 11 spoons."

"I don't understand."

Ziechlech replaces silverware into the empty drawer. His wife bends down to help him. He hands her a spoon and a knife. They stand up. He spills the drawer onto the floor again.

"Dad!"

"How man—"

"12, 11, and ten. You missed a spoon and a knife. They're probably under your big fat foot."

Madison looks at Ziechlech.

"Shit."

"Yes."

"MOMMY!"

"Ok. Ok. Let's try something else."

"This is the fifth time in five minutes she's exhibited eidetic memory."

"Eidetic memory is an urban myth."

Ziechlech deadpans at Madison and slowly raises an eyebrow. His wife whatever waves him off.

Ziechlech opens a drawer. He pulls out an unopened pack of drinking straws. The label says 28 colored straws. He shows this to Madison then rips the plastic off.

"Diz, how many?"

He flashes a fist full of straws at his daughter who rolls her eyes.

"Seven."

His wife raises her eyebrows. "You see, it's—"

"Blue ones." Dizzy slurps her tea noisily. "Mom, I do this all the time. Look," she hops down off her stool and trots around the kitchen.

"Nineteen silver handles, eleven buttons, thirty one pearls, forty six freckles; there's thirty-eight books in the hallway library, 81 stars in the picture of the ship in the den, fifty-five stinky old men named "Svichya" in the poster of the Brest historic council that's in the hallway by the door, seven umbrellas, eleven door handles—five brass ones—and Mr. Kriek is finished sailing."

Ziechlech looks out the big window behind his girl. Their crazy distant neighbor is indeed docking his craft. Dizzy never looked out the window. He didn't even see her glance at the lake.

Her mother gathers her up and razzes her nose. She walks into the den and looks at the painting of the Alert, an antique three masted cargo vessel. She counts the stars. He daughter counts out loud.

"I only count 65 stars, Diz"

"In the sky, duh. But there's 16 more in the painting."

"What painting."

"In the little room on the back of the boat."

Madison peers into the painting, into the captain's quarters, the windows are barely an inch on a side but the painter managed to squeeze in a lot of detail, including an early American flag, 16 stars carefully rendered in it's blue field.

"How long have you been counting these stars?"

"When we walked through the hallway the first time, for tea."

"What about the doorknobs?"

"I've been counting them my entire life, mom. For *years* and *years* I've been counting them."

"Dizzy, you're five."

"Yeah, do you know how many times I've counted the doorknobs in this place?"

"I bet you do."

"547 and a half times."

"Half?"

"I only counted them once today."

"Once—you count them in the morning and in the evening?"

"When I wake up, when I go to bed. Doorknobs, handles, drawers, books, shoes, umbrellas, how many times Dad says "For the love of," letters. I ran out finally and today I decided to count stuff that's in stuff."

"The stars."

"And stinky old men named Svichya."

"I knew you could *read.*"

"Oh I can read anything."

"But the counting is impressive."

"I know! It's massive!"

"What else?"

"I count how many times you say Shit."

"Dizzy."

"You say it a lot."

"I do not."

"When you're working with the guys on the wall, you say it all the time."

"How many times today."

"Well, I was with Dad most of the day so far but before I left your office you'd said it fifty-two times before I went to lunch."

"Shit."

"Fifty-three."

SKIN

[Found html document: instructions for joining the game, "Skin"]
Call 44-937-639-7546.
[Found audio doc. Response call.]
"You're in."

LIAR

Viglund Bogr is a liar. His lie is cartoon evil bad. Black. Drippy. Hackish. Because of his lie, he has become a billionaire, his fledgling company sold to the highest bidder for more money than any one man can actually ever spend. Here's how.

He set up a website, a scanned pdf page, an online document with a phone number. If someone called the phone number, they heard a voice say: 'You're in,' then hang up.

He did it as a joke. Put it up then started posting comments on social sites about 'the game'. He was carefully vague. He was vaguely vague about a thing that was ephemerally nebulous.

rockstar322 says: I hear that once you join you can't un join.

fantastic5 says: urban myth.

fantastic55 says: really? Call this number (888)

rockstar322 says: Holy shit, did I just join skin? WTF!

And it caught. It sparked. It enflamed. Vig made the phone number charge one dollar. In three years he was turning 3.5 annually just from calls and 31 million from advertising. He had no staff. No product. Legal fees, some. But mostly he just tooled around with no one knowing who he was: the guy who invented Skin.

Skin is the most popular game on earth. There are no stated rules. No profiles. No email letters (officially) and no time limit. There's no objective. No play. No way to win. Because it doesn't exist. Officially. But as nature abhors a vacuum, the virld abhors irrational humor and people who made the call imagined they had joined a global network of players all controlled and managed through their scrolls and skull buds.

The game was fueled by paranoia. Wrong numbers were 'instructions,' spam was just the central game master 'checking in.' People began to use Skin as a scapegoat for their worst ideas. They caused a little mayhem. Here and there. Some graffiti. Some augs. Some bomb threats. It got a little weird. Sure. It spiraled out of control and some government guys stopped by and Vig's lawyer had to run through some hoops and it took a long time to explain to these government guys, more than mildly paranoid as a matter of profession, that the company was a phone and a single page.

"I swear," Vig said, in the bare white walls of an office in Oslo. "I was going to make a porn site but I'm from Sula and there's not many girls there."

It scares the crap out of him. He sells the company and goes awol.

But a game that doesn't exist can't be eliminated. Or controlled.

Players begin to develop rules. Someone creates a new phone number, this one with two lines: one for leaving instructions and one for receiving them. People begin to assemble points systems and ratings and profiles and soon there's a micro economy and soon there's an industry and soon—

"We've been skinned."

"Son of a bitch."

"Yeah."

"How?"

"Fuck if we know. But some of the shit going on in the lab is not in the operations manual. Someone's banking points off us. And check this out."

The guy clicks a button and an mp3 says: *Infiltrate the Api Nomada.*

"Son. Of. A. *Bitch.*"

"We're tracing it but really, seriously, we'll probably never be able to figure it out on that end. We have to watch for anomalous behaviors and new goals and action tangents that are semi radical."

"Semi radical. That's like saying someone half sneezed."

"Well, yeah. Really. We've got a horde of wildly creative people pulling this circus in nine different directions at once to solve problems most of our clients didn't even know they had. We wake up radical. We eat and drink radical. But imagine someone trying to get points in Skin; they're going to come up with a creative idea that's unoriginal. It'll have to dovetail with their instructions or their play or their strategy. It'll be creative but it'll be rigidly creative."

"I don't get this game."

"Imagine a self-aware urban myth you can play."

"Major."

"It's like mold. By the time you notice it, there's so much you have to call somebody in."

"So who do we call."

"Gypsies."

"I'm in a fucking cartoon."

"We call in an audit. They get into everything and find out who's fucking the dog. We call them up, they come up with a name, we cut them a check. EZPZ."

"Fuck. Click it."

Two days later, they're sitting in a room with Cable Toje.

"This is itchy." Janice Borgan says this with her arms crossed. She's the elder in legal and she runs contracts for the Api Nomada. She wrote the contract separating Toje from the main Armada to start his own, the *Nash Equilibrium,* with the presumption they would take on the large audit jobs and partner with the *Api Nomada* on large-scale efficiency audits, leaving the *Api* with more room for creative problem solving and visionary work, while the *Nash Equilibrium* ran capture programs and game boxes to find the little things and squeeze the bugs out of a company. The idea was, they'd leverage the very next big time customer onto *Nash* to get them started.

"I just didn't know it would be us."

"So you're Skinned."

"Appears that way."

"I don't play."

"That's a contractual requisite. You and everyone in the *Nash.*"

"That's a tough one. Gaming is personal. This is going to come up in our investigation of the *Nomada.* If a person is playing, are they allowed?"

"Toje, seriously. This isn't the supreme court. If they're playing on *Nomada* time and equipment, then they're violating."

"Yeah, but we don't—I mean you don't—ok, we don't really have a schedule. It's not like we're nine-to-five. We work all the time, we play all the time. We're fully merged."

"We've worked on the division of work and PT. People know the difference. I would say that any action, any decision, which clearly indicates it was made in favor of scoring in Skin violates. Any person involved in Skin has to make everyone around them aware."

"Like a gold star on their chest?"

"Fuck you, Toje."

"Look, Skin is more culture than game. They feel sovereign."

"Do we need to fab out a new bathroom sign?"

"We're looking at 823 million players. They never sign off. They never quit. It's part of their lives. I'm telling you the game was aptly named."

"They should not be making decisions that are priority Skin."

"It doesn't work like that."

"I thought you weren't a player."

"I'm sympathetic, but not involved."

"That bodes poorly for the contract."

"Why? I think it would be better. I'm less prone to make a scene."

"Granted." Borgan whips out her scroll and drops it on the table between them. She calls up boilerplate, adds a couple of points, deletes an entire page, spins it around to Toje.

"I don't have legal."

"Well, you'll just have to trust me."

"So I'm in?"

"You're in."

"Irony."

"I expect a lot of that in the near future."

###

[Virld transcript. In-game comm proxy. virld transcript notes: gol=go offline; WAM= wait a minute; tf?=the fuck, indicates disbelief; vid=viddy, indicates look, from custom map origins, 20th century novel: *A Clockwork Orange*]

<v 3467-88 dkick t door/v>

<v 3467-34 rufkm? /v>

<v 3467-88 tf? /v.

<v 3467-34 vid bee /v>

<v 3467-88 ru allergic? /v>

<v 3467-34 ... /v>

<v 3467-88 tf? /v>

<v 3467-34 WAM! />

<v 3467-88 okok, nocaps, dude! /v>

<v 3467-88 ... /v>

<v 3467-34 [perimscan set; virtcamoflg ext: 32; door=not] /v>

<v 3467-88 specs n ur nbox /v>

<v 3467-34 got spex. tf? v/>

<v 3467-88 door specs /v>

<v 3467-34 yykk ... /v>

<v 3467-34 ... /v>

<v 3467-34 ... /v>
<v 3467-88 [perimscan rboot; virtcamoflg ext: 0; door=not] /v>
<v 3467-34 gol! /v>
[virld transcript; comm. convo from above; post capture; IDs assumed]
0: Is this shit real?
1: Hell yes it's real.
0: We're playing a custom map! I fucking built this map!
1: Dude, my mom's got a language gate on this line so we have to watch it on the comm.
0: I built this map! How'd they get in here?
1: Sfucking beast.
0: Dude!
1: Sorries.
0: I'm going in.
1: Srsly. No.
0: I want to vid.
1: I don't. Dude, these guys are topline. I'm outta here. Move over to your scroll.
0: No fn way.
1: Ok. Let's hit it.
[Virld transcript. In-game comm proxy. virld transcript notes: hs=holy shit; os=oh shit; WAM=wait a minute]
<v 3467-88 k /v>
<v 3467-34 k /v>
<v 3467-00 Hi. /v>
<v 3467-88 OS! /v>
<v 3467-34 HS! /v>
<v 3467-88 Hedsets! /v>
[virld transcript; comm. convo from above; audio post capture; IDs validated]
0: You see that?
1: We're meat!
One and Ziro, in the game, hyper muscled and overgunned, are looking at a door in a custom map they designed that they didn't design. Standing in the open doorway is an illuminated woman of unparalleled beauty. She is blue transparent, her hair dreadlocked and cascading into a brilliant azure robe. On her forehead, the symbol of a honey bee pulses with a silver glow.
3: I like your mod.
0: How'd you get in here?
3: I can't tell you that.
1: Dude, this is tricked out.
0: What's in that room?
3: We're having a meeting.
0: In my mod?

1: I don't think we should talk to her, hommebucket.

3: It's alright. Your mod keeps all the comms offline.

0: you could make your own mod.

3: We're kinda paranoid.

0: Who'd be tracing you to a kid's shitty mod hack.

3: It's not shitty at all.

1: Dude.

3: Proximity is an issue for us so we have to meet virt. Like everyone else. But since we're working on stuff that's really sensitive, we can't take a risk of being tracked. Not now, or ever.

0: And my mod is on a card and my machine is off net and my dad makes me shut it down at 11:30 so this room disappears at bedtime.

3: Bingo.

1: So, wait. You're telling us all this so—

0: Who's gonna believe a 12-year-old gamer had a convo with a Sub Nomada avatar?

1: Equals Bigfoot.

3: I'd like to think I'm coming across a shade less hirsute.

0: There's, like, ten million hack mods.

3: Yours have great detail.

1: You've been in our mods before?!

3: [in-virt-screen generation, parse 135/987 display session 333243: note: game replay shows 3467-88 dive into an office mod followed by a targeted swarm of gunbots. A trash can pops its chrome lid, reflecting the targeting lasers of the frontline enemy bots, initiating a fusillade of friendly fire, racking up a nearly self-perpetuating rolling thunder score for 3467-88].

0: I remember that.

3: I couldn't help myself. I'm surprised reflective camo isn't used more in that game.

0: It will be now.

1: Legend.

0: So why are you talking to us? Why not lurk?

3: We're interested.

0: In?

1: Don't like it.

3: We were wondering if we could influence your design just the tiniest little bit.

0: For?

1: Ten Geckjillion dollars.

3: We were thinking more along the lines of some very subtle influence in your game tech.

0: Like?

1: Fifteen Massikeptilionbajillionquadrillion dollars.

3: How's better equipment sound?

1: New Decks?

3: We represent someone who represents someone who represents someone who does gaming hardware testing. Interested?

1: Yes.

0: AYK?!

3: Nope.

0: What do you need?

3: Altitude.

VEGAS

Vegas. Say it and know what it means; it's like Paris or New York, a city that built its name and is defined by it on the flop. Splined out across a low ridge in the Nevada desert, a jewel of lights, photographed by more vacationauts than any North American city. Even Dubai can't keep up with it for decadently ludicrous architecture, for experiments in cement and fiber gone bad, for lost parking lots, for hulking shadowy garages gone to weed and taken over by raving punks and whore gangs, for the sheer wildness of its tech, an invisible army of iris readers, fingerprint cullers, and a million and nine ways to capture your brush.

For all that, it is a city easy to disappear into. Never dim, a place with almost no shadows; even the garbage cans are illuminated.

Cable Toje lies face-up on the front seat of his car staring into a blur of lights, drinking Kane Break, straight, his feet hauled up onto the ancient vinyl dash. His scroll is draped across his abdomen, limp to conserve. His hair is falling over his ears. His beard is wild, the hairs just coming to the point where they'll give up their urgent poke out of his weathered face and fall down and stop stabbing him in the nose when he sleeps. His eyes are swimming in a rheumy pink of tears, tiny tide pools of regret for leaving the Api Nomada. His official promotion and bump to senior elder partner in a new Armada was a joke, a sham, a cover up for being ejected. Let go. Thrown overboard.

"They made me walk the plank, those fuckers."

"Car?"

"Yes?"

"Take me to the collectors."

"Sure thing," the car drifts onto a side street, finds the highway, and heads south. Toje feels the difference in the wheels and props himself up to stare over the dash. He slides all the way up in the passenger seat. He pours his drink over the side, noting in his infinite spreadsheet mind how much money he just wasted on a dark celebratory toast, and looking behind him quickly, the sheen of it disappearing. He slides over behind the wheel. Flicks it onto manual.

"It's important that I note your current sobriety."

"Go fuck yourself, Car."

"Language."

"See you tomorrow."

The car's auto system shuts down. Toje feels a subtle change in the way the wheel responds. The computer dies and the car comes alive. It flexes in his grip, strains to uncurl, the engine seems to growl low in its throat. Toje comes alert in quick degrees, drops the pedal and the car surges forward, the traffic adjusting like water, a dim illuminated ribbon appearing on the highway as a kind of asphalt overture which Toje ignores. He glides through the traffic against the judgment of the road, drifting aggressively between fleets of delivery trucks, moving vans, roving party cars with tinted windows, sleek selachimorphic limos; longbikes. The highway notices his recklessness and adjusts velocity, trajectory, fleet management, communicates 10 miles in both directions to give this crazy fucker some open road and Toje finds himself cresting a butte with ten empty lanes a mile fore and aft and he howls to the open sky, floors it. The car arches it's back and leaps forward, its enormous glistening azure hood playing a neon blur of starlight.

He's clocking 132 when the collectors loom over the horizon. He makes it in nothing flat, slows down, stops in the middle of the road. He stands up in his car, perches on the window ledge of the passenger seat and pours another Kane Break neat. He's just breathing it in when the traffic surges past him, two lanes away, perfectly poised, like he's a feature. He picks out the different projects at the collectors through a flicker of cars like an old movie, frame by frame.

It was their first job.

The *Ghost Ship Armada* came together in a coffee shop in Lisbon. A bunch of highly skilled remotes traveling and working together decided to make it official and sold their collective skills in designing an impossible water collection plant in the desert. Cable Toje ran numbers and models. His spreadsheets and open sourced modeling became instantly famous, with everyone from highly paid MIT professors to a 7th grade science class in Danville, Illinois running his models with their favored parameters to find the best way to irrigate the sands.

The presentations and live model nodes were called Bloom. People crushed it. They had to ramp servers three times. The advertising alone made them millionaires. The final design was an ornamental jewel, an architectural marvel, the eighth wonder of the world. They not only collected water, they altered the local ambient environment. Scientists and advocates went ape but they all had to shut up when average rainfall overclocked Santa Fe, Albuquerque, and plants poked their little green heads out of the sand. Lakes formed. Fish appeared. Half the city drove out when a flush of wildflowers around the collectors streamed live.

The great benefit, though, what Toje was so proud of, was the response to the *Ghost Ship Armada's* collection of skilled designers and labor camps. They had no fixed location, no building, no home address. They built a temporary hanger on property and set up shop. They worked in bars and casino restaurants.

As a joke, they referred to themselves as castaways and somehow the vernacular grew to cover, a metaphor born from their intense gaming mindset. The analytics crew was the first to name their group, like a ship, taking the metaphor all the way to call their leader Capt. Cable Toje. They named themselves the *Carroll Deering,* after the infamous ghost ship found abandoned off Diamond Shoals in 1921. They made shirts. Their badges identified them as crew of the *S.S. Carroll Deering.* They referred to their rented cars as "landing craft." It got out of hand in a good way, turned into an institution. A useful metaphor was born. The engineering designers were the *Caleuche;* the fluid dynamics team the *Zebrina;* the climate physics team became the *Merry Celeste.*

These metaphors gave life to the crews, gave them identity and cohesion where walls and department wings would have done so in a legacy corporation. They called themselves co-ops at first but that hippy simile died on their lips. They were not broke. They did not live lives of sweaty aggravation. They made bank. Most of them already had plenty of cash to start, living as well-paid remote workers in low budget but semi luxurious digs here and there as they traveled the world. They were gypsies without wagons.

They'd pick up a job, swing into town, rent a big house, and hire a cook and cleaning crew. It was fantastic. They spent a lot of time smiling.

In Vegas, they found a new trick. Big engineering jobs spit out patents and technology like government research mills. They spun the collectors' tech out all over the globe, turning Bahrain into a veritable wetland. There were streaks of new green in the Grand Canyon. NASA had their tech on Mars.

Local impact was carefully orchestrated to increase what they referred to as in-pocket for the ordinary citizen. They only took the job after the City of Las Vegas Water Department promised it would deliver the water free of charge to locals, based on profits from shared patents and tech spun out of the project.

The day Cable Toje put on a monkey suit and ceremoniously drank a champagne flute of clear H2O on the floor of the Trump, he was pulling down 4M a year and looking at a bonus.

But they were already old and cranky when they started. They'd lived a buckshot delicious life and after eight years putting together the collectors and drowning in a sea of cash, most of them hung up their laptops for retirement. They had enough money to splurge on their individual obsessions. Butler became a fucking Luddite hippy nomad, doing free art, and telling stories. Tosh created a little paradise of no-tech, bought a trailer—a fucking trailer—and grew expensive dope. Two others got married, bought houses in lux green-zone paradises. One of them went sky and floats above it all in zero g. One of them bought an island off the coast of Madagascar. And Ziechlech, fucking Ziggy, fucking bastard. Z took their economic tools and went home, opened a business, and wouldn't open source his code.

It pissed Toje off to no end that Ziechlech wouldn't share his tech. He was their financial department, the *Pride of Baltimore*. His weirdgenious way of visualizing micro and macro economies made for an easy pitch to Vegas as a way to pay for the collectors. But it was a way of visualizing he'd come up with alone, headphones plugged deep into Jon Hassel and Bach, weird fucking smile on his face, pscyllicibined into a couch, ignoring the rest of them. He never really, really, joined the armada. He paid his dues. He made them ungodly amounts of cash. But he never told them how. His tech was his tech and when they all shook hands and split up, he took his tech with him and headed back to Eurussia, to Belarus, to the frozen lake where his family had lived since Dracula's dead granddad, and made twice as much money and more. He became an economy of one. And he matters. And Toje secretly hates him, even though he stood up at the wedding, even though he introduced Ziggy to the wan and deliciously, bristlingly, alarmingly intelligent marine geologist who bore his only child, even though Ziggy, a man who seemed to have one, maybe one and a half emotions, turned in the Vegas hospital with his screaming bundle of skin in his giant Belarusian hands, weeping with joy, and said to Toje, *Be her Godfather,* even though, he still hates Ziggy, deep down, under the manners and the toasts, he hates him because he was the first to leave and because he inspired the rest to do it and most of all, the real reason, the core cause, is because Ziggy didn't play ball.

Hide his daughter. Fuck. Toje swirled the rum in his glass. He held it up and watched it bend the towers at the site, flickering through traffic, a sepia newsreel, a nickelodeon of regret.

"Car."

"Yes?"

"Take me to the Monastery."

"You are in a zone requiring proper—" Toje slid down into the passenger seat and belted himself in. "Thank you."

The car moved slowly forward, traffic parting around it like rapids around a rock. Toje felt a gentle nudge as the nav tech hooked into the highway and he accelerated into the flow, finding himself between a translucent artist's studio where a man slept peacefully in a hammock between a hanging bench and an unfinished nude, and a cross country lettuce farm.

CODE

Ziro Hamahachi is 16, codes at the kernel level, has mod permission on a couple of global scale open course games, and brings home a 3.9 GPA. He takes out the trash, realigns the solar tiles, trains the dog, and recently calibrated the walls of his house so they respond auto to whomever is in the room, with a priority overlay that favors his mom over his dad only because his mom has exquisite taste and his dad always makes the damn thing pick out old dirt bike video stills and game play. When Connor walks into the living room, the walls reformat to clear, playing his neighborhood in real time from externals. It freaks out the dog.

Today he's slumped in the couch watching a Mai Lai slaughtervid when a UPS drone lands on the porch, beeps twice, leaves a small crate, and jets off over the roof. Connor gets the box, peels it open. He unzips an inflated pillow and pulls out perfectly white earbuds. No logo. No R or L. It looks like it was baked in a kiln. He pulls out a case. Inside are six months of display contacts. He pulls out two sleek, white, ceramic finger rings. He pulls out a tiny envelope, wax sealed with the image of a bee. Inside is a card with a smiley face drawn in blue ink.

Connor goes quietly ape shit. He puts it all on, the contacts giving him shit but he gets them in. The earbuds fit perfect. The rings resize and talk to each other in a burst of nanoflash. He looks up and through the translucent walls of his house. There's a card hanging in the air in front of him. He reaches out. He can feel it. He runs his fingers over the raised letters and feels the transient bump beneath his fingertips. He feels the ridges of his fingerprint scrape over the edge of the stiff paper. The letters spell out THANK YOU and beneath that, {press here} which he does.

He's in a blank world.

If he stares hard enough, he can see his house and consequently his neighborhood through white limbo.

"How the fuck—"

There's a woman standing there with him. She's dressed in a lab coat, holding a clipboard.

"I'm Laura. Ask me anything."

"How do I code?"

"There's a coding assist embedded in the drive. You just start building."

"How do I do that?"

"It's a voice activated, hand manipulated, full immersion real time walk-through environment simulator we rigged-up for a job in Bologna."

"It's so good."

"Isn't it? We decided to keep this one to ourselves for awhile. You're using my old rig."

"This is Beta?"

"Oh yeah."

"Are you real?"

"Simulated here. But I am plenty real wherever I am. Shall we get started?"

"What's the trigger?"

"Hands together, Master Ziro."

Ziro brings his hands together. A pair of ghostly brackets float before him.

"Give me a one acre workspace."

Connor is standing in a bright field. He walks forward but remembers he's in his living room so he grabs the visual edges of the field and pulls it past him so he ends up in the furthest end of it.

"Ray trace—"

"Fingers together."

He taps his fingers together then draws a box. It floats wire frame. He taps the wires to create new manipulators. He turns it into a mailbox.

"Trick."

"It's adaptive. Don't think too hard about it. You'll learn. It'll learn."

"What did you use this for?"

"We grew a bridge."

"How long can I keep it?"

"Yours to keep."

"Beast."

"You're welcome."

He tries buildings first, but they're riddled with holes. He tries mountains, mountain ranges, cliffs, jets, a space station. Nothing captures his fancy. He feels like he's running a line and he is. He keeps a global scan running in a loop to drain attention and it picks up a run of pipeline villages from Mumbai and he has it.

He starts with a logging balloon, sews a few of them together around a biodiversity platform from a national G video, and rigs a platform. He builds Zeppelins, turns them vert to create sky pillars. Wipes it all. Starts over. Builds a high altitude research station, then dupes it then reskins as an abandoned high altitude research station, slings rope bridges between them, grows weed forests, staggers come-to-Jesus trees here and there, dangles roof gardens in old two liter bottles, creates alcohol stills, uploads a culture, populates it, gives them autonomy, skills, tools, and soon has a paper shack slum in the clouds.

He is lost for days.

He breaks the windows out of the bridgehouse. Trails vines down the side. Underneath he cakes the glass of the observation bowl where he's started keeping his desk and rig, and where he spawns each day to work.

This room is hyper Victorian, an inverted conservatory gone to seed, full of old books and wild birds. He picks here to spin out his fantasy library/office/game room.

Three weeks later, Ziro appears in this room after school, after chores, after walking the dog, and the blue woman is sitting at his desk. She is accompanied by three others: a skate punk monk, the Egyptian goddess, Bet, and Elvis Presley. They see Ziro as a floating stellated rhombic dodechahedron.

Elvis: Platonic solids much?

Bet: That is a beautiful avatar.

Blue Woman: Ziro, how delightful.

Ziro's avatar floats dead center in the room. There's a 360 degree view through multi paned observation windows. They're standing on a gas polyhedronic substrate floor so they appear to be floating a half-mile above Florida's Atlantic coast.

Ziro: Well?

Blue Woman: Ziro, it's beautiful. Really, truly gorgeous. Your detail is beyond and your adherence to your visual theme is, well, it's beyond.

Bet: I love how dirty everything is.

Elvis: Except the observation decks. The glass there is perfect and this floor is trick.

Ziro: From every other angle it doesn't even exist. Just a solid steel sub deck with a bunch of donculous pipes and cruft. Even if you were detailing, you'd pass right over it. In truth, it's a lens.

Elvis: We're in a camera.

Ziro: And a projector. I can project false military onto the ground to draw fire, intimidate.

Monk: Only military?

Ziro: Anything. Anywhere. We're geo stationary. As the map rolls under us, our focal point stays fixed. However, I can fix that focal point, even though we drift off. And the library of structures is pretty much the set of all real things with motion and reaction.

Monk: Care to demonstrate?

Ziro: Sure. I run everything in real time with real weather data and Google earth stats. What you see out the windows is exactly what's happening now. I upload municipal holo stats so even the traffic is real time.

Ziro's avatar spins on its dorsal axis. They are all looking down onto six miles of beachfront from Daytona north. There are bulkheads of cumulus building southward, stalking toward them in the afternoon tropical heat. They drop suddenly toward the earth, the great floating collection of gasbags and swing bridges groaning when they stop. Even the visiting avatars bounce gently.

Now they're looking down on a high school football arena from 800 feet. Ziro's avatar's pectorals rotate. A jeep enters the arena followed by a string of elephants and two more jeeps. There are trainers, a school principal and attendants, and busty cheerleaders.

Elvis: Looks like they're getting ready for a rally.

Bet: Maybe we should wait.

Blue Woman: They can't see us.

Monk: They're the demo.

Elvis: Sonofabitch.

Bet: Worthy.

Blue Woman: Ziro, I am impressed.

Ziro: Plus, they're AI skinned so. . .

Ziro's Avatar whirls. A voice crackles out of the speakers in the room.

Voice: Smith.

Ziro: Can you move the elephants to the north end?

Voice: Roger that.

A man peels off from the group in a golf cart, waving and radio chatting. They hear the chatter as the crew routes the pachyderms to the away endzone.

Voice: How's that?

Ziro: Arm and launch.

Voice: Will do.

The crew loads gargantuan saddles onto the animals, then great swiveling Gatling-gun rockets. Each elephant takes a rider, crouches, then launches into the sky, coming directly at the observation deck.

Ziro: Light up the bridge.

The elephants hover around a hanging bridge, firing rockets and 50cal incendiaries until its burns to a cinder, and falls away.

Monk: Why the elephants?

Ziro: I like elephants.

Bet: And they're hard.

Ziro: Yeah, that's true. It was really a pain to get that to work. Even with the stuff you sent me.

Elvis: So, we can fly this thing anywhere and observe in real time with collocation and zoom.

Monk: And rocket firing flying elephants.

Elvis: And rocket firing flying elephants.

Ziro: Pretty much.

Blue Woman: Ziro, what do you want to be when you grow up?

Ziro: Elephant trainer.

They all laugh.

Bet: Alright. Ziro, if you'd show us how to use this room?

HANG CITY

Ziro walks through the inverted world. The streets are hung with gondolas hung with gourds, fruit, data kits, wireframe models, scree of every dork that's glommed onto the city. He walks on a narrow root bridge grown between the central core and a side spoke, looking for a bhang walla that just opened. A man floats into view, plopped into a ballooning cart, jetting a thick brown stream from one cup to another and calling out to Ziro. He hands him a mug with data steaming off its surface. Ziro glances down into the cup, his Japanese John Lennon visage cavorts on the shimmering surface: Ziro's new predilection for Gatsby flash.

He's wearing a strawboater with a black band, a cream linen suit with the faintest blue stripes, a gold vest, a starched white Oxford without the collar, and no tie. His glasses are perfect golden circles, Winslow specs, with a saddle bridge. In his realapartment, Ziro carelessly reaches out to his fab pot for his morning cup of bhang. As he brings the mug to his lips the sensation of doing it and his illustration's flawless animation merge; brief vertigo.

Hang City is his baby. He is defacto Mayor, gatekeeper, architect, and star. He built Hang City from blank, from swishes and genuflections of his new trade: digital architecture.

He started with the observation deck at the core but when he was finished and the bee people moved in, he couldn't stop and they never said word one about him grafting a slum onto their new digs. It grew out from the center in perfect imitation of leaf rot and mold, a vaguely spoked lumping of digital hovels, long corridors, stately reproductions, junked cars, enormous warehouses with a single couch in the middle. One guy from Burbank reproed the VAB building NASA used to keep their rockets in. Its all held together with old vines and twine and steel cables and rust. You can fab anything you want. He left the code out on the wires. But you couldn't decide where it ended up. The neighborhoods were random. There were emerging themes. People really seemed to like the look of slummage so a lot of the structures were tin roofed, tin walled, bambooed, and often open sided.

What they wanted was peace. They just wanted to lounge back and chill in the quiet of whatever structure they'd culled together from wireframe chuck and jpegs and grit. Ziro made scripts that aged their work. He had a dirt script and a script that flung old leaves and debris. He wrote spider and beehive scripts.

Someone threw a script so you could overlay your local map onto your AR local map and walk through a mall with the visuals of walking through Hang City. Some people drove like that. Soon enough the whole thing mushroomed out of control and occasionally Ziro would go avatar and flit up to the top of the center spire and look around at the massive Sargasso of digital scrum he'd accumulated. It was worse than Sims or any of the second life scenarios. People lived here. There was commerce. They linked transactions to realife actions. People worked here. It had taken less than three weeks.

He was meeting One for cruft inspection which pretty much meant they were going to fly Hang City in real time noting the highlighted structures where there was tangled code that needed to untangle.

Or, as One called it, tag.

One dropped out of the sky onto the root bridge next to Ziro. They bumped mugs.

"High as fuck already, ain't you Ziro."

"Yup."

"You ready?"

"Yup."

"OK, well, let's not grow old or anything."

In the dappled sunlight coming through the wickett overhanging bridges, One grinned at Ziro and fell backwards into the open air. One stepped off and, taking a timid sip of Bhang, fell feet first after him, his clothes not even rippling.

They fell through a briarpatch of root bridges and hanging vines, catwalks and open decks, gaining speed. Ziro, peered down through his specs at One's feet, one having opted for the full effect, clothes snapping in free fall, hair streaking behind him, face rippling in the force of his descent. Ziro gained just enough speed so the soles of his feet settled gently onto the upturned soles of One's and he thought tag.

A junction below them blossomed into wireframe and numbers and they stopped just above it. Ziro followed One's steps perfectly so they walked mirrorform around the construct. A bevy of assistants spun around One like Disney cherubs as he spoke his notes and delegated jobs and fired off a quickie to the architect about his code.

Ziro hovered just above One as One spoke with the tenant's avatar, highlighting wireframe issues and suggesting technique. He duped a few assistants to help the guy regrow his apartment to form. He spent a few minutes training. Ziro looked down through his feet and noticed Hang City was flying again. Every once in a while the Bee people would move Hang City's locus. They did this in oddball real time. One noticed Ziro and joined him, looking down at the highway rolling underneath.

"Why real time?"

"Floco."

Ziro sipped long on his bhang. "I mean, we can just plug in numbers and boom, we're there. Why do they actually drive the fucking thing. And it reacts, look at that shit."

They tracked a stream of cruft and debris falling out of the sky until it blipped out about 300 feet off the road.

"Trick."

Ziro watched the highway.

"Fuck me. They're following someone."

"Again, total goofballery. There's ten thousand ways they could track anyone, anywhere, anytime. Why do it in real time and why do it from the deck of an invisible sky slum?"

"I would go with the invisible part. And maybe they can't use any of the noted 10K spyware methods because ..."

"Because?"

"I'm thinking."

"Gamer logic."

"This is a quest."

"Side quest."

"No, this is main. And if they use spyware it lights up."

"So what? They're the Main."

"Or not. Maybe they're watching—"

"Spying!"

"Spying. Not their quest."

"Not even their game."

"NPC"

"I don't know. This is tangled. Let's find out who they're looking at."

"How do we do that?"

"I was thinking invisible spy plane."

"Kind of fast."

"Zeppelin."

"Steampunk much?"

"Skysubmarine."

"Dude. I'm on it. Gimme five."

Five minutes later, after ransacking the LOC for framework, and modding their new ride, Ziro and One stand on the deck of a gorgeously rendered Sen Toku class I-400 WW2 Japanese mega sub, as it descends toward the highway.

"There's no data streams to highlight, they're just using your real time stacks to look at whatever is below Hang City."

"So we look too."

"We're at the edge of their visibility cone, locked in with Hang City. What do you see?"

"Traffic. We're headed north, bearing west. There's ten bajillion cars."

"You could lock onto any one of those cars and not have to think about it."

"Yeah but they aren't doing that. They can't. For some reason, it'll give them away."

"Or it'll give away the mark."

"But how? Every car down there is hooked into something. The data streams are massive. How would anyone notice one more?"

"So," Ziro shelves his empty cup IRL; on the Sen Toku bridge, he reaches out and it disappears. "Our benefactors are using an invisible sky slum to follow someone, but they don't want anyone to know they're following this someone and a simple nearly transparent data stream would give them away."

"How would a data stream stand out in a forest of data streams? I mean, if you lit up the streams coming off the highway . . ."

One is good at this shit. He downloads a DMV stat lens and every car on the road is suddenly stellated with data rivulets, long trailing upstreams and downstreams, the highway itself now a pulsing corridor of data. Bright lines leap into traffic from billboards and advert nodes, pulling facial data, checking interior stats like temperature, occupancy, and age. The cars streak along the highway in perfect coordination, all of them exactly the same distance apart, zooming off exits, zooming through intersections, all of it with perfectly boring precision, all of it a perfect forest of data spikes. Except for one.

"Jesus. Look at that."

"Maybe their GPS is busted."

"There's not a single . . . look at the ad streams, they're just bouncing back."

"Who's in it?"

"Rastafarian and a monk."

"That's normal."

"Dude is 10 and 2."

"Not possible."

"He is. Hands on the wheel, eyes forward."

"But look at the traffic, it's right up next to him–no avoidance."

"I think there is avoidance. But not much."

"He's hiding."

"This is our guy!"

"Srsly, a Rastafarian and a Monk? Suspicious characters."

 "We've located a plot."

"Hero or villain?"

"I would ask the bee people but now I'm scared."

"Yeah, which are they? Right now, they're looking slightly villainish."

"But we know they're good."

"Best disguise for a villain."

"But they're doing this too."

"What?"

"They've got to light up the data streams. It's the easiest way to follow these people."

"Rasta boy thinks that by visually and physically blending with traffic, he can disappear into the motoring stream. He's trying to smuggle something. And he's wrong."

"Right. Those cars are reporting him, or trying to. Every time he bumps into their space, it sets off an alarm which reports 'a [blank space] intruded on our margins."

"Someone has to be checking that out."

"Maybe. But people are allowed to drive, right?"

"Emergencies. Dirt roads. Blue line highways."

"Blue line?"

"Legacy. My uncle showed me on a paper map. Mapmakers used to print local two lane roads as thin blue lines. Connector roads, old logging roads. Paved. Wiggly. He said bikers preferred them."

"No maintenance. No tech."

"No records."

"How long can a manual car travel on an autohighway before they violate."

"Forever. It's legal, just stupid. But the other cars will tag it. Pretty soon they'll shun it, send those stats to all the cars around. He'll be obvious."

"So not violating but known."

"Yeah."

"So recorded."

"Well, recorded by being not-recorded."

"So someone will have a search on for a blank space traveling north."

"If they're smart."

"How smart is Rasta boy."

"Those dreads have power."

"Years."

"So he's old. And he's doing this."

"So, smarter than us."

"Smarter than us."

"So we're prime directive?"

"How many Hang Cities are there?"

"One."

"No. There's an infinite supply. Every person in Hang City is looking at a virtual of it."

"Virtual virtual."

"Right. So the guy in Omaha really has his own Hang City which perfectly replicates the source City and every other user's Hang City and all changes and blahvium infinitum."

"TED much?"

"Can we have a Hang City cut off from the main?"

"You mean a franchise?"

"Fuck. It's ours, right?"

"I think it belongs to the Bees."

"Yeah, but they're like, silent partners."

"Very silent."

"Dammit."

"We're idiots."

"Your dad does love him some mocross."

"Either they're assassins, they're blackmailers, they're hackers, or they're rescuers."

"Or something."

"Or something. Whatever it is, it's secret and it's focused on Bob Marley and the Dali Llama who are manually piloting an antique vehicle on main roads to avoid detection."

"We don't know that. You're Sherlocking."

"What else?"

"We don't know the motivations of the Bee people. We don't know the motivations of the Rastafarian or the Monk."

"Right. We need to divide them. So, logic problem."

"Brain boner."

"Bee people. Rastaman. Monk."

"Cartesian layout."

"The Bee people are scary capable yet they hired us to build their scope."

"Equals evil."

"We don't know that."

"Suspicious."

"Nshit. Rasta man is hand driving a rusted truck through autotraffic."

"Equals ninja."

"Well, physical skills and nerve you only get through training."

"And old."

"So legacy ninja."

"Marine? Conscript?"

"I'm going with some version of guard."

"But who is he guarding?"

"Cargo?"

"So him and the Monk are trucking something non-tech."

"Non labeled."

"The Monk is the only passenger in the equation so far. He isn't performing an action. Not driving. Not pursuing."

"That we can tell."

"Logic problem. It's not a known until it's a known."

"Ok. Let's take a closer look at the Monk."

Ziro types a message to his crew and the Sen Toku sends out a drone. They receive video from the facial recog streams from fifteen virt boards, all of them showing the occupants of the truck.

Ziro leans forward. "Fuck me, it's not a Monk."

One snaps a still, a close up with incredible definition. The Monk is glancing over at the Rastafarian, cheeks stuffed with food, chewing happily and trying not to laugh at, presumably, a witticism from Herr Rasta. The Rasatfarian's eyes are crinkled into a smile that practically splits his head open. They both stare at the still, seeing the Mohawk is a wig, seeing the way the sarong falls over Dizzy's chest. Seeing the cut of the chin and the cheekbones and—

"It's a girl."

"Cute girl."

"The plot, it thickens."

"So The Bee people are secretly watching a highly trained Rastafarian smuggle a cross dressing monk over the open road."

"And we're helping them."

"So we can x out evil for the Monk."

"We don't know."

"Whatevs, One. Look at her. She's like 17. She could be our sister! Not evil."

"She's cargo."

"So Bee people are undetermined but highly capable and I say suspicious."

"And Rastaman is undetermined but highly capable and I call suspicion."

"But the Monk is neither and is cargo."

"So what are we?"

"Fuck, One. I think we're heroes."

Vat Sushi

[Jones] and Tosh slide into traffic as sunbeams pound through the gaps in the St. Augustine skyline. Tosh drives with oily precision, keeping his rusty old truck perfectly centered between autonomous cars. [Jones] leans her head against the side glass and stares at the woman in the car before them. It's an articulated Olds, jacketed with pinions and sockets and as the sun comes up over the rim of the world, it paints the white car pink and warms [Jones]'s face and she comes alive a little.

The woman in the car before them is kicked back eating breakfast with chopsticks from a bowl; she's online with someone and laughing her ass off. The Olds is a teacup car with a circular bench all the way around, little console in the middle. Lady's got her feet up on the console. She takes a bite and rolls it around in her cheeks and catches [Jones]'s eye. She holds a beat then barks an order and the windows mask into a saver, making it look like the Olds is filled with sea monkeys. Tosh chuckles.

They hit Cordelle, head west on 280. Tosh unrolls the solar bed to charge up so they don't get grounded in Georgia. Tosh has the old roads like a library in his head; old asphalt ribbons avoided by living cars for their lack of embedded tech. If you drive these, you have to pilot your vehicle. New responsive roads track them over and beside and through like a bracken of chrome and extruded concrete with locals whizzing along, just the tops of the cars visible, 130 miles an hour, blurred by speed and precision. Zooms along through a necklace of lost towns, Americus, Cussetta, Pittsville. They merge briefly in Ft. Benning but drop off the terrifying luge of the autohighway asap, cutting around Opelika, Dadeville, and stopping for roadside barbeque under a kudzu cathedral in Alexander city, long abandoned and weed choked, its mental hospital and shopping malls home to drifters and chrome freaks.

Tosh takes them on side roads, county roads, and cut-throughs, skirting below Nashville city and pointing across Kansas and Oklahoma to the Nevada border.

They pick up road food–jerky, candy, farmers market fruit and nuts. Sometimes they scoot out into the robotraffic to come through a drive thru. Tosh favors Marley's, a Jamaican jerk joint chain he curses endlessly before and after his load of meat pies and champagne colas. [Jones] prefers Sushi Bowl. Tosh dismisses it as fake since they're too far from the ocean to be real. He calls it Vat Sushi.

The closer they get to Vegas, the less [Jones] eats.

25

Something happens in Vegas.

GATORLAND

The monks take her on a high-speed rail to Kissimmee, FL with a ticket for the side worlds—Parrot World, Snake World, Monkey Jungle, and Slam Pants Planet, the whole sordid sub-DisNiversal junket. The bus leaves them in front of a giant concrete Alligator's gaping jaws. The teeth are three feet long. The Monks give her a tiny back pack with some gear, including a contacts rig that IDs her as Jamyang Gephel, Assistant Events Coordinator for the North Nevada Buddhist Temple and Skate Complex, age 23, most recent ziploads: Among Tibetan Texts: History and Literature of the Himalayan Plateau, and Double Nickels on the Dime. She activates her complimentary tour glasses and a cartoon alligator appears in the foyer leaning on the teeth, speaking flawless Tibetan with a southern drawl. She has no idea what it's saying. The idiot guide's voice becomes background as she walks around the macabre gift shop loaded to the eaves with teen gator skulls, baby gator skulls, gator feet, gator teeth necklaces, gator foot ashtrays, and whole taxidermied adult gators raftered like Neolithic zeppelins, then down the slight ramp that takes them below the waterline of the gator pool. The monks crowd the glass, the drone of the avatar disappearing into their murmur. [Jones] stares into the murk. Shafts of solid sunlight pillar and fade into the coffee brown backwaters of the pool. Gators swim between them in lazy ophidian arcs. She imagines she's in the nave of a drowned cathedral at the end of the world.

She is startled by an albino gator that swims into the foreground. All the other gators have become wallpaper but this one is a comet. Orange and yellow and mottled, it is the instant focal point and the crowd's murmur grows to meet it and [Jones] realizes they're murmuring in North African dialects and glances over at the crowd to see the Monks are all gone.

"Fucking ninja," she says to nobody.

[Jones] runs out through the teeth into the parking lot, now occupied by a swarm of cars piled into the northwest corner, a fleet of busminivans with green and black North African Shopping Tour logos pulsing around them, and a legacy pick-up truck with it's hood thrown open sporting a cursing Rastafarian hanging off its grill like a swollen tongue.

Jones looks back into the gaping jaws of the zoo. The North Africans are shopping in a frenzy, laughing loud raucous laughter at the gator skull ashtrays and picking gator rib meat out of their teeth with sharpened gator claws. They trickle out and their busminivans come to greet them at the teeth. They're all gone in a few seconds, leaving [Jones] alone in the sun. The cartoon alligator steps into her vision saying something in Tibetan and waggling his fingers in front of his snout. She rips the tour glasses off and tosses them into a bin painted to blend in with the three-foot teeth.

The Rastafarian crawls out of his truck. He's staring into the engine. He looks up and stares at [Jones].

"[Jennifer Maria Jones]?"

[Jones] is startled but she doesn't acknowledge the name.

"[Jennifer Jones]!"

[Jones] turns to look dramatically behind her, then pantomimes 'me?' The Rastafarian shakes his head, long heavy jeweled dreads shaking and jangling. He whips a cardboard sign out of the cab with [JENNIFER MARIA JONES] scrawled in sharpie black. He walks quickly over to stand next to [Jones], then holds up his sign as if he's waiting on someone.

"Ziro, wait—" he pulls a pair of flat-black Raybans from his dreads. Puts them on. Stage whispers, "for effect. Your limo awaits."

[Jones] rips her backpack off her shoulder, whirls and slams it against the glass doors of the gift shop.

"Fuck this!" She tears off her shitty Mohawk wig and throws it through the teeth into the bushes. "It's hot as balls. I'm worried about my dad. I want pants." [Jones] drops into a puddle of girl. Sobs. Tosh reaches down to help her up. [Jones] scrambles away from him.

"Fugoff! I don't know you!"

Tosh tosses the cardboard sign into a trashcan (an embedded milky screen displays .11 credit but can't connect to anything to transfer the funds so they go to one of 50 charities associated with the company that picks up the trash, Kenyan Waste Disposal Distribution Dynamics; .0956 of that shifts into the credit stream of the CEO, Muthoni Wanyeke, who is notified in her upper right hand screen as she's looking out the window of a busminivan passing back by Gatorland after hitting a Sweet Maria's drive-through just up the road to check on it's visuals (she owns that too) and get a decent cup of Kenyan coffee; she sees a nearly empty lot with a Rastafarian and a pissed off monk arguing in the gaudy teeth. The Monk hightails it out into the lot. Muthoni clucks her teeth and shakes her head, "Takes all kinds, mama.")

"[Jones]!"

[Jones] turns around, hardly losing momentum, practically whirling, and charges back at the surprised Rastafarian truck mechanic. A clerk comes out of the Gatorland gift shop with a plastic gun pointed at Tosh.

Tosh puts his hands in his pockets, whispers "motherfuckleshit," to himself.

"Sir, I don't know what's going on but I am prepared to tase." The clerk is a Mombassa import sporting a nametag with Jomo engraved into the plastic. Tosh and the flood of New Kenyan immigrants don't get along too well. The New Kenyans are rich, deeply racist profiteers who grew up highly superstitions about American blacks. They think they all have direct roots to slavery and gang warfare. Tosh has been called Kunta, porch monkey, and slave more than once and he's touchy about it.

The man picks up on Tosh's reserve, the hands in the pockets. He thinks Tosh is scared. This poor Mobassian man has no idea Tosh is a millionaire expat from the Armadas who ran their security crew and could probably break the man in half with his eyelids if he wanted to. He put his hands in his pockets because some shit just happens instinctually when a gun is pointed in your face and Tosh didn't want to hurt the guy. So hands in the pockets. But the guy pushes the taser a little too close.

In an instant, Tosh easily snatches the yellow pistol.

"Give me back my taser, babu!"

"Rafiki ndugu," Tosh slips a plastic card from his shirt pocket. It flashes $200. The Kenyan fixes on the card. "I am having some difficulties with my adopted daughter. She runs away. I come get her. The same old story. Wasichana, yeah?"

The Kenyan takes the card and glares after [Jones] who has stalked dramatically to the highway and turned north.

"I will leave the gun in the ditch by the road."

"See that you do, babu." The clerk goes back into the store.

Tosh jumps into the truck. He catches up to [Jones] and paces the truck along the road. Busminivans and botcars zip around them. [Jones] ignores Tosh for a good 50 yards of hot asphalt and waves and waves of killer Floridian heat. Tosh is playing a weathered mix tape with the windows down. He fishes a can of pop from a slurry ice and water in an old beat-up styrofoam igloo. When he pops the top, the sound is deafening. [Jones] glances over at him, sweat running down her neck. He's got his head tilted back, gulping an ice cold R.C. [Jones] stops. Tosh hits the brakes. She hears creaky leaf springs and junk roll up in the bed.

Tosh kills the tape player.

"I have more, child."

"How do I know you're not a perv?"

"Why do you trust the monks and not myself?"

[Jones] shades her eyes and squints up the road. There's an outcrop of autostores and ridethroughs a half mile up. In this heat, by the time she gets there she figures she'll be dead. She gets into the truck.

"Thank God," Tosh rolls the windows up and cranks on the air. "I thought I was going to burst into flame."

"How do I know you're not a perv?"

"Lady, my tastes are refined."

"What does that mean?"

"I'm not into Monks."

"I'm not a—"

"You're not a monk. No. But who are you? I don't know. I know you are under the protection of my friend, Dr. Cable Toje–"

"You know my godfather."

"–who told me only that I would be picking up a lonely Tibetan from that hideous zoo and that the monk would be staying with me until further notice. Apparently you are in some kind of trouble big enough for that—and I'm being diplomatic—frugal bastard to call in a favor from the Nevada llamas to dump your sorry, skinny ass at Gatorfuckingland, and instead of gratitude you almost get me tased then make me sweat balls for a mile and a half. And now you think I might be a pedophile? I hope your guest etiquette isn't as rude as your holy-shit-I'm-being-pursued-by-assassins etiquette."

Tosh slams the tape back into the player. "Fearless Vampire Killers" roars forth. [Jones] sinks back into the hot naugahyde and sulks. Tosh drives through "Big Take Over," "I and I Survive," "Right Brigade," and

"Jah the Conqueror" before he pulls off the highway onto a dirt road with tall weeds on either side. After a few neglected pastures roll past, Tosh pulls into the Whispering Pines, a dilapidated trailer park. He stops next to an immaculate 1956 Spartan Executive Mansion. He fishes the taser out of the door well, hands it to [Jones].

"If I strike you as the least bit pervish, just point and squeeze. I'll go down like a sack of hammers."

He gets out. Walks into the trailer. [Jones] can see him fussing around in the kitchen through the massive windows at the front of the trailer. She gets out. She comes in.

"Fine. But I need pants."

THE API NOMADA

They've rented a house on the Dalmatian Coast, taking a job to remove a WW2 era dam, reverting two thousand square miles of lake into the primeval forest it was before 1939. But the dam is also a very useful bridge. Lose the lake, keep the bridge. It's a three year job, involves intense legal wrangling and real estate efforts, ecotechtural work, long range forest randomizing, undergrowthing, highway design, rezoning, mass material reclamation work, job relocating, company relocating, home relocating, community repurposing, politics, and plumbing. People living on the shores of a beautiful lake will now be living on the edge of a canyon. They have a daring design to move all the houses to a similar point on the river after everything settles down. They'll even retrosculpt to make sure the homeowners have a nearly identical view to their previous perch. Computer models suggested homeowners would not be happy. The computer models were correct. Politics have entered and the job is shut down.

"At least a year." Georgia Bradshaw is slumped into an antique leather chair running the tips of her fingers over the decorative studs lining the face of the armrests. She's pissed. But she's trying to maintain. Her specs are running her favorite ambient, a morning street in Prague, shops opening, coffee vendors talking to the florists, a dog barking on a balcony. It's far in the background and zooms up easy as her blood pressure mounts, until she closes her eyes and she's in it, standing there sipping a strong cup of Brussels café au lait, seeing the pink sky turn blue. Her BP recedes like a tide and the ambient fades out with it.

She opens her eyes.

"At least a year. And then it's a restructure for a year to adapt to new terms. We're two, two and a half years out from breaking ground. I'm shutting it down."

Her number two is leaning against a desk. Her name is Susan Ling. Her very close friends, people who worked with her back in the day, call her by her original @ handle, "sling".

Sling says, "Vegas?"

"Yeah, but something else." Bradshaw waves the windows opaque, flitters her fingers in the air punching in a code that squelches the room. "Z called."

"Must be pretty cold in hell."

"Somebody's fucking the dog."

"Kind of goes against the whole one-man-band thing Z advertises."

"We roll with the extra clever: Someone found a way to steal."

"How bad?"

"He's writing a press release."

"Fucking hell."

"Want to read it?" Bradshaw opens a page, floats it over to Sling.

"How much are we down?"

"We're covered so it doesn't matter. Shit, the truth is, Z's covering every loss. He's just announcing because he's so fucking professional."

"So nobody lost any money."

"Well, they did, but Z covered it."

"And he's plugged the hole."

"With scorpions and lava."

"So no future danger."

"Nope."

"Yet he's going to announce."

"Yep."

"Fuck me."

"It gets worse."

"Mrs. Z?"

"Dizzy."

"No way, Brads. No fucking way."

"She's fine, Z put her in castle."

"Well shit. What?"

"The people protecting her kind of lost her."

"Nshit—WHO!?"

"The Merry Celeste."

"That crazy fuck."

"Well, maybe Cable Toje had something to do with it—and Tosh was driving."

"Fucking Pirates."

"Sling, we gotta get in there."

"Where is she?"

"Nobody knows. She went off grid."

"Those guys live off grid."

"Not Cable."

"Ok, let's get a team together."

Sling claps her hands together asana style. In her vision, a shared bank of screens appears in mid air. She fiddles and the leader boards for the Api

Nomada come up, a calendar of faces, all available, stats scrolling in their info box. Bradshaw pulls up her own screen, a glowing turquoise globe with crimson points and lines arcing through like flight paths. She fiddles, subarticulates, gets a map of the current Api Nomada locales. There's a trend of flight lines from the Dalmation coast to rural Spain.

"Some food festival. They're insane about it," Bradshaw says.

Sling pulls together a lineup. Shares it with Bradshaw. They delete some, argue about a few more. They pull from puzzle gamers and strategy freaks. One girl who is their current go-to for real time stats and hard science. An anthropologist pattern maker. They get five people and bring them up private.

"We need to find someone. A Founder's daughter. She was supposed to be under protection and well hidden, just disappeared."

"Protection from?" It's the statistician.

"Bad guys, Jane. Who the fuck else?"

Z ANNOUNCES

Ziechlich and his crew leave Illinois Masonic. They hop into a stretch that's really a rolling conference room, drive to O'Hare, get on his jet, and launch into the sky. They're already over the Mississippi when he dials up the PR screen and adjusts his tie.

In Vegas, a guy in a lavish suit is in the middle of a sandwich when his screen wipes right revealing Ziechlich fussing with his four-in-hand. The guy freezes, eyes locked on the screen. His system is geared to auto play anything regarding Ziechlich's company, Ziechlich, Madison Zichelech, or anything remotely having anything to do with the money streams entering and leaving Ziechlich's zone of influence. He watches as Ziechlich tells the world how his finances were tapped, what he did, and everything is fine. Then Zeichlich names the perpetrator, a man of some public recognition, a man who does not play well with others, and to whom the guy in the lavish suit is more than somewhat obligated. The screen wipes left, replaced by a grid of financial reporters all going exactly the same stratospheric level of ape. The guy gives a 'huh,' finishes his sandwich, then starts talking to his room.

THE BLUE ROAD

The skysubmarine dips its nose a little as it follows the Rastafarian and the monk. Ziro and One are at the helm in full exaggerated Japanese naval dress uniform drag. One sports a monocle. The great windows of the Sen Toku bridge display the legacy truck tooling down the highway.

"Alarm."

"What?"

One points at the passenger side indicator.

"Legacy tech. Didn't you ever play GTA? That's a blinker."

The truck disappears.

"Fuck! I told you!"

"What happened?"

"It's gone. Hell the road is gone. It's just advertisements and 'sorry' tiles."

###

Dizzy wakes up from a fitful nap against the door of the truck as the wheels bump over the exit ramp and onto a sidereal. They head toward a small village of ridethroughs.

"Captain Orioles, I'm not hungry."

"We are leaving the highway for good, stowaway."

They pass through the village onto an open road.

"Why on earth?"

"Well, I'm old and my ass hurts and I want to walk around a bit."

"Noted."

"I also want to teach you how to drive."

"Unnecessary."

"Not if we want to make Vegas on time."

"Cameras, brushes, facecogs—"

"We're on a dead road, Stowaway. There's no commercial value because there's no real traffic. This is legacy blacktop. Might as well be dirt."

They pull over into a kudzu cathedral, a spent Marathon station, some guy has a truck nearly identical to Tosh's, the back loaded with a beautiful display of melons, corn, and baskets of heirlooms. Tosh lopes over to the guy. Dizzy explores. Kudzu has perfectly skinned the building, the pumps, the overhang. She looks down at the pavement, great cracks outlined with gray, rusted bottle caps peeking out from the vegetation, legacy glass bottles dusted and dull, a dead plastic sign gone to mold. She finds a boat hidden in the weeds, its former red gloss deck pinked and cracked, seats blistered and split, listing to the side and full of dirty brown water and leaves. It's like a tide pool. There are water bugs and spiders; a single hyacinth lily with its edges turning brown floating by the skeleton of an outboard motor. Dizzy catches a flash of frogskin.

"Diz."

The guy's split a melon on the tailgate and Tosh is holding out a slice, deep salmon by the rind, a glistening yellow where the flesh thins out at the slice; she can practically feel her teeth biting into it, juice sluicing down her chin, when Tosh is slammed back into the pile of fruit, a bright crimson cloud where he was standing.

The fruit guy explodes into furious movement, throwing the melon at Diz so she's already off balance then he sweeps her up and hurls her under the boat. She rolls into the steel trailer frame, bangs herself badly. The guy zig zags back to his truck as bullets track him, a red dot appears on his bare shoulder and he whirls back toward the cab. He ducks wild eyed behind the doorframe.

Diz scoots backward under the boat, spiders scuttling away, dead leaves and plant gook all over her. A lipstick drone zips in and stops directly in front of her face, hovering perfectly still, its propellers little blurs in her vision over and under the cylindrical body. She is rigid with fear, paralyzed, all her thoughts, all her attention focused on the tip of the drone.

The guy bolts across the tarmac. He zigs toward the pumps. There's a huffy farting noise and he's peppered with red splotches, spaz dancing into one of the pumps, falling hard onto the cement.

A heavier drone descends into view, a giant gun with wings, solid fab plastic blue, its cylindrical body pregnant with ammo. It moves over to the fruit truck and opens fire, a Gatling gun chain of bullets. It shreds the thin rusted metal of the truck, reducing the fruit to a haze, Tosh's body jerking in a red haze, the stream of ammo moving carefully, diligently back and forth in a deafening sputter, the truck falling apart in chunks, until nothing is left but metal bones. It goes on forever.

Then the blue gun turns toward Dizzy, floating closer until its bulky frame pushes aside the Kudzu leaves and the hot muzzle hangs only inches away from Dizzy's nose.

A tiny mechanical voice: Follow me if you want to live.

Dizzy crawls toward the gun as it backs out with its lipstick companion. She glances over at Tosh, motionless, dreadlocks scattered out over the pavement. The gun leads her to the side of the road. A legacy car comes around the curve just as she walks onto the pavement, a long white limousine. A door opens.

"Ms. Ziechlech."

Dizzy only stares, her eyes darting to the blue hovering gun. It suddenly zips away, silent and fast, as does the little one. Another vehicle arrives, also legacy, with men pouring out of it. They fan out across the kudzu covered gas station, subvocalizing and pointing. Two of them grab Tosh, carrying his body into the gas station store.

"Leave him alone!" Dizzy leaps toward them, but bullets tear into the pavement between her and the men. "Fuck!"

"Ms. Ziechlech."

"FUCK!" Dizzy roars at the man, her face turning beet red, nails digging into her palms. "FUCK!"

"Ms. Ziechlech, you have to get in."

"I am not getting into that fucking car. I don't know what's going on. I am not getting into that fucking car. WHAT IS GOING ON!?"

The man whispers something forward. A gorilla of a man, vat grown, game boss architecture, steps out of the driver's side, opens the man's door. He gets out and the gorilla shadows him as he walks around to Dizzy.

"Ms. Ziechlech, I am kidnapping you. You can get in the car and shut up and play nice, or I can have my driver break your arm."

"FUCK YOU!"

The driver steps around his boss, grabs Dizzy by the wrist and snaps her little finger. Dizzy screams. He piles her into the car, scream sobbing. He buckles her in. They load up, drive off, the gas pumps going up in flames behind them.

The partitioned glass slides open enough for the vat man to toss a chill bag into Dizzy's lap. She lays her broken finger into it. A painkiller vapor stick follows.

The Man opens an armrest, hands Dizzy a cold blister of water.

Safe Harbor

Ziechlecj walks into a vault. Six other people trail behind him. They are dressed in simple belted robes, with no phones or scrolls or clips. Their contacts have been assessed and approved. There is no recordable tech in play. Two of them carry thick college ruled legal pads and black Ticonderogas. They all take seats on comfortable benches. In the center of the room, a giant scale model of the Edmund Fitzgerald is bathed in an LED approximation of dappled sunlight.

"They say it was a rogue wave that sunk her." Zichelak runs his fingers along the glass over the topside of the tiny ship. "There's a fore bridge, engines and crew bridge aft. In between it's all deck, all made for holding taconite pellets. If a rogue wave hit it and shifted the pellets, the ship could have rolled. Nobody really knows."

"Mr. Ziehclech, if we could talk about our accounts?"

"Of course." Z waves his hand over the protective housing, a diamond hard film comprised of billions of bacteria-sized nanobots all having joined hands and locked their arms and refusing to budge until Zeichlech's floppy wave releases them; they blink out like a soap bubble, flitting invisibly into the microscopic trough below the ship, revealing the actual model, which Ziechlech touches with obvious relish. He strokes the Fitzgerald, rubs his fingertips across the blade-like edges of the smokestack. He hums quietly. Tunelessly. Then he steps back, comes to attention, and rubs his hands together. He steps forward and with a sense of ritual, lays his finger on the very nose of the prow.

"Your accounts start at €734,983,432.47." Ziechlech looks up at two accountants who dutifully record the amount. His hands travel down the port side of the hull to the anchor chain. "Account 1 carries a balance of €3,456,652.19," his fingers take the tiniest leap to the anchor chain, deftly grasping the first link. "Account 2 carries a balance of €834,914.07 . . ." Z continues and the accounts fill the notebooks line by line. When Z finally reaches the stern and doles out the final account, they only have a few pages left. Z stares at them. His stare is barely interrupted by a CFO who brings him a small cup of espresso from a machine near the back of the vault. The accountants and a different CFO take advantage of a table near the model. Z never lets them out of his site as he sips his espresso and wanders to the other side of their table, watching them draw complicated geometric grids of transfer and recursion and percentile drift. An hour later, they have rewritten the accounts on the right hand side of each page, with notation. They take another 45 minutes in a line-by-line comparison of the notebooks. Ziechlech glances at his intern who produces a tabletop shredder. One of the accountants, a slim MBA of indecipherable gender from Sierra Leone, hands her copy to the intern who feeds it whole into the shredder which minces the notebook into confetti which whirls in a tube before being incinerated in a quick puff of hot smoke. Ziechlech takes the other notebook. He returns to the bow, lays a finger on the lip of it, and replays his ritual, laying, in his mind, the new contents over the old map of their accounts. When he has finished, he hands the notebook to the accountant, repeats the new amounts from the bow to the stern, then incinerates the notebook. And the pencils.

The bots join hands to recover the Edmund Fitzgerald. Ziechlech's interns silently open a smaller vault door then push the entire display inside. They lock the stainless steal vault and spin the circular handle.

Outside the vault, Ziechlech's client's party disappears into private changing rooms. He walks into the meeting room at the end of the vault chamber. The CFO comes in immediately, still knotting his tie.

"What if we had our own?"

Z has waves in his notary. There is a pile of documents to sign and seal, proving to the world and all banks and brokers and financiers the transfers and shifts are legitimate and insured by ZID Financial.

"A Mentat?"

"Yeah. Like we brought in our own guy. One of the accountants."

"It wouldn't work."

"You can't be the only guy in the world who can do that."

"No. There are 27, currently."

"You have a failsafe."

"I have a method of protection for my data."

"You mean personal encryption?"

"There is a mistake."

The CFO stops fixing his collar and stares hard at Z.

"Our figures aren't right?"

"The figures I give to my clients contain a carefully distributed error set."

"We pay you for perfection, Z. I did not know—"

"You have been my client for 3 years. You have never experienced a loss or mistake from the account records I maintain for you, correct?"

"Perfect. But--"

"Carefully distributed. Think of it as a key. If someone tries to send in a mentat to record everything I say, if they don't have the key, then their figures will be incorrect."

"But that's exactly what we do!"

"No, I give your accountants the key."

"What if you're making all this up?"

"Well, I make a lot of people rich by making all this up so if I am making it up then who cares?"

"Is it always a ship?"

"Always a ship."

"Why?"

"I wanted to be a pirate."

The CFO stares a long time at Z. He adjusts his watch band. Others come in. Z meets and jokes quietly. He shakes hands. The CFO and the accounts sign actual paper. Everyone leaves.

In the car on the way back to their offices, the CFO keeps thinking about Z. Eventually, as the landscape blurs past and the traffic swarm fills his view, the music from the Pirates of the Caribbean ride at Disney pops into his head and he remembers the cool air and the hideous cheesy foot of the animatronic marauder dangling off a bridge as he glided beneath. He imagines that robotic countenance as Z as the foot lands on his face.

Vegas

The limo slides into Vegas as if it's coming from black and white into Kodachrome. The colors are relentless. Overwhelming. The hippest architecture in town is a squat cube of a club called "Offswitch" with flat black paint and no external illumination. Dizzy stares at it as they roll past, a solid hunk of dark in a roaring, exploding, city of blinding light. An absence. It resonates. She presses her palms into her eyes and falls backward into a memory.

St. Augustine. She's in school on The Merry Celeste.

"Well I just don't fucking understand why playing invisible chess makes a fucking difference is what I fucking mean."

Yeats is perched on a stool smoking a coffee-mug pipe. When the breeze settles, he disappears in a blue cloud.

"Well I don't fucking care if you don't fucking underfuckingstand. E4E5."

"Sure. Take my fucking pawn. Nc6 . . . white develops and defends."

"Bb5 a6"

"Big surprise. Once again, having played this same fucking game for the 900th time, I am not at all surprised that you have taken my bishop. Congratufuckinglations."

"We've played 14 times."

"Eternity."

"I have a reason."

"I am unFUCKINGfathomably curious, Captain."

William Butler Yeats shifts on his stool and the legs creak beneath his whiplike frame.

"Why in the world would I play the same exact mental chess game with you twice daily?"

"You abhor sanity?"

"Diz."

Dizzy envisions the chessboard in her mind. Over days of playing, she has turned the board into a life-sized castle courtyard set, with live figures for each piece. They have names, quirks, mustaches. In her mind, all the pawns ceremoniously turn their backs on Yeats, bend over, and drop their pants.

"I'm thinking."

The Merry Celeste is moored in back of the Oxford behind a short wall overgrown with wildly ambitious Bougainvillea. A waiter brings them grapefruit slushies. Yeats notices the salt on his rim. The bartender poured him a Salty Dog. He winks at the waiter who nods and disappears. Dizzy gets up and follows the waiter back into the bar, cold air like a solid block of ice, and takes her drink through the big glass front doors, down the walk past the kite store and the Old Lady, down a path between two houses and out to a private walk with a bench that fronts the ocean. She watches the clouds, tries to see dolphins; she watches a helium skier fly off the waves and up over the city, feet churning wildly.

A man walks out onto his porch in a pair of shorts, a big floppy hat on his head, sunglasses screwed on tight. He sets a martini down on his deck rail, then hefts a bonsai tree alongside it. He waggles his hand and Blue Rondo sweeps out of the living room through the open sliding glass door. He glances at Dizzy over the top of his shades. Dizzy cocks her head and digs the music. He watches her for a minute as she lets the music set. Then he turns back to his tree. He stares for a moment then suddenly goes after it like he's giving it a mean haircut. Dizzy rolls her glass in a little evaporating ring on the railing of the walk. She glances over at him again. She's absorbed.

It's a windswept thing. She has no idea it's a *Juniperus procumbens*, a dwarf Japanese evergreen. To her, it is a tree growing on the edge of a cliff, fighting the wind from day one. The bark is twisted and gnarled, warped into a vision of arboreal pugilism. Shades keeps at it then picks up a hair dryer and blows the debris out of the shallow pot and off the back of his porch. Dizzy sees the tree on its cliff. Fearless. Defiant. Then she clocks out and smirks out at the ocean. For second it was a movie. Classic suspension of belief. Marveling, she wonders how many hours Shades has devoted to creating this little freak of nature. He's there now, bent over with a pair of tweezers, carefully picking cruft from between the stones in the pot.

If you could somehow rewind this tree, then every moment of effort, every knick, every twist, every piece of plucked fluff would unspool into the mind of Shades. Somehow, that tree is a recording—

"Mother fucker." Dizzy plops her glass down solid. Shades looks up. "Nice fucking tree, Shades." He nods his head slightly, goes back to tweezing. Dizzy spins on her heel, walks back between the houses, through the OED's glass doors, sets her glass in a plastic tub near the kitchen, walks right out the back across the lot to where Yeats is snoring in his hammock and kicks him in the ass.

"Jesus Haploid Christ, Diz."

"It's a recording."

Yeats grabs the pole behind his head to steady the hammock. He looks down his sundrenched lanky beef jerky chest at Dizzy with the sun behind her hair like a bomb.

"Some kind of information storage. Code."

Yeats reaches down for his grapefruit and vodka. The ice is all melted and floating on top. He sucks it all down. Licks the salt off his lips.

"Now we're getting somewhere." Yeats reaches up, yanks on a line of twine stretched from his hammock pole through the kitchen window. There's a faint chime. The waiter peeks out. Yeats holds up two fingers then makes like a gun. The kid comes back with two bullitos. Yeats takes them on a wire spool table from back in the day.

"We are not random."

"You ride a wheel to tune your gravity harp. You're named after a sunken boat. You define random."

"No. Nothing is."

"Yeah, ok. I took physics. I call bullshit."

"Sure. You're right. But you're wrong."

"Oh good, a lecture on dyslexic indeterminism."

"The universe is a infinite swirling gyre of total random insanity. Endless potentialities exist, duplicate, self annihilate, mirror, and fade out. At the subatomic level, reality is a crapshoot."

"Einstein disapproves."

"Strings, rings, half flotons, full flotons, semi hadrons—they wink and twinkle like stars. You can't clock 'em. You can't predict them. You can't even actually observe them. But zoom out by a billion and you have this cup of coffee," he tilts his cup, takes a sip. "From the quark POV, this cup of coffee is an entire universe. A possible universe. From the QPOV, nothing is determined. All the sparks and sizzles might end up being my espresso. *Maybe.* So, yeah, you're right. But you're wrong because fuck all that, this is a cup of espresso and it was made by some guy," Yeats downs the coffee, turns the cup over. Faint blue ink reads Baleek; "in Ireland. There's no question about it being real—even though from the QPOV, it might just wink out of existence at any second."

"But, chess."

"But, *patterns.* This cup is not a cup. It's a *pattern.* At the Q level, there's more of it that is *not* existing at any given moment than *is* existing."

"Schroedinger's cup."

"But try and believe that."

"Yeah, it's cute but I don't really care about it." She sips her espresso.

"Zoom out. The whole world is like that. Everything is just whirling paths, jungles of habit.

"Chessssss."

"How do the potentialities at the Q level which might become a coffee cup become a coffee cup?"

"Some guy in Ireland?"

"Yep. Some guy in Ireland. He takes a lump of ceramic clay and molds it into a cup. And some other guy built the mold. And some other guy dug the clay. And some other guy . . . as we go, we keep affecting the Q level potentials so they skew more and more toward CUP and less and less toward DIRT until the Q level sparks and sizzles fix in a pattern that stays CUP until anger or entropy determine otherwise."

"So, chessssssssssss."

"Your chess game is a pattern without meaning. It hasn't resolved into a cup. It's still a lump of clay. It's data."

Her pawns masturbate furiously at Yeats.

"Dirt is data. A cup is meaning."

"How exactly?"

Yeats walks over to his caravan, pulls open a cabinet door, and yanks a worn out cardboard box with a faded full bleed close-up of a chess board, big white Queen in the foreground. He opens it, sets up.

"Let's say you wanted to have a conversation about coffee. But you didn't want anyone to overhear you so you and the other guy use the board and the pieces to—"

Dizzy quickly distributes a handful of pawns on the edge of the board. She looks up at Yeats with a blank look on her face.

"Quick. But I don't know the order."

"Of course you do."

[The pawns are lined thusly: **C1 A2 F3** and **E4**.]

"Café."

"Por favor," she says.

Yeats reaches up and yanks the twine. Chime. Peek. Bullitos.

"Ok, so I've been learning spy code. That's great. I have a couple problems. First, I can only chess-spell through H; second, I'm not a spy."

Yeats doesn't say anything. Dizzy sips her espresso and eyes him over the rim.

"Mother *fucker,*" she whispers.

"Bingo."

###

The Limo slides into a parking garage. They get out, get into an elevator, and go down. The doors open into a factory of some kind, which they breeze through like they have background music, onward through more doors into a spacious apartment with a monitor wall playing an infinity pool by the Mediterranean. The old man offers her a couch, walks behind a desk. The vat grown man stands behind Dizzy. She has not seen him eat or drink for two days.

"It's my place in Portugal," he says, waving at the wall behind him. "I miss it."

"I'm hungry."

The Old Man stares at Dizzy for a blink.

"Maureen," the Portuguese wall shimmers and a woman is standing there. "get us some nachos and coke."

"What the fuck is a nacho?"

"Mon dios, child, where were you raised?"

"And a sushi plate. A martini," he looks up at the Vat. "And a shake for security."

The woman fades out. Seconds later two men in white kitchen uniforms roll in a cart piled high with multiple version of the order. One of them sets a chilled glass on the Old Man's desk, shaking a stainless shaker vigorously. The Old Man watches critically as the martini is poured, just a degree away from freezing, into the glass. They leave. Dizzy snorfs the sushi like a starved cat.

She has observed the following: this guy has a fuck ton of money; this guy is a douche bag criminal; this guy grew up poor and has something to prove. No class. She throws a shrimp carcass on the floor and wipes her hands on her shirt. She can see his nostrils flare.

Prawn to shrimp five.

"Maureen," his computer generated secretary appears. "Bring in the ship."

Two other guys come in a few seconds later, pushing a display cart displaying a giant model of a boat. Dizzy keeps her cool, but she knows this boat. It's the Defiance, a two-masted schooner that sunk with no loss of life after running into a bigger ship on Lake Huron. She knows the cargo, the name of the captain, and how many boards make up the hull.

"The Defiance." She peels another shrimp, dropping the cold legs into the couch cushions.

"So you know this boat," the Old Man is impressed. Excited.

"I dived it."

"Your father is fond of it?"

"He's way more into the John J."

"They sank together."

"Shit happens."

"Stop being churlish."

"I don't know what that means."

"You were raised by the smartest people in the world. You know what everything means."

Zing.

"How did you get dad's boat?"

"I didn't. It's a replica."

"It's a good one."

"How do you know?"

"The scrollwork on the bow is exceptional. That's tough."

"What does it mean, Ms. Ziechlech?"

"It means you bought your kit from a reputable dealer, probably one of my Dad's guys in Belarus."

"True. But I mean what does the *boat* mean?"

"It means boat."

"Ms. Ziechlech."

"Tell me about the trailer park you grew up in."

"Ms. Ziechlech."

"I don't know what the fuck you want. It's a fucking boat. Why are all you old fuckers so obsessed with boats?"

"That's exactly the question."

"Well obviously I don't know the answer. Now you've kidnapped me, even though my dad went to STUPID ends of the earth level shenanigans to hide me and you fucking killed Tosh so even if I DID know anything, I won't tell you."

"Grammar."

"Nazi."

"Freud had his insights, Ms. Ziechlech. I need you to tell me what this boat means. I too want to know why all those old fuckers are obsessed with boats. I want to know why your friend's ID had him listed as *Captain Aurelius Tosh.*"

A cold shaft of horror drops through her.

"That's his fucking name."

"He wasn't a captain. He was a security consultant."

"You're a clerk."

The Old Man purses his lips and glances up at the Vat Grown Man who reaches down and flicks Dizzy's hand. She screams.

"Take her to her room. Give her the boat."

And so there she is looking at but not seeing the Defiance in a nice room with a throbbing broken finger and a hole in her heart where Tosh once smoked copious amounts of ganj. Oh man could she use a hit.

Like he's psychic, Vat comes in. He holds out his hand, palm open, and waits. Nothing happens. He looks down at her busted hand then pops his fingers twice in the universal come on signal. Dizzy stands up. He very gently takes her hand in his gargantuan skillet paw. His other hand reaches into his jacket and returns with a slim plastic purse. He lays the purse into his skillet hand, slips the tips of his fingers into it. There is a pink glow from within the purse accompanied by faint whirring. He withdraws his fingertips then nods gently to Diz. She removes her hand.

"Nope."

Vat reaches out and very gently takes her by the wrist, and very gently holds her damaged hand over the purse. He lets go, holds his hand for a moment to make sure she stays. Then he lays his fingers against his lips, commanding her to silence. He touches the top of her hand with his fingertips and very gently guides her hand down into the purse.

She feels a dry liquid, a dense gas. The light from the purse flares to a bright red and the pain in her finger fades a little. She starts to pull her hand out but Vat touches her hand again, very gently, and keeps it there. The purse light fades to a peachy color. The pain disappears and the gaseous dry liquid warms suddenly. Relief pours through her body. Vat reaches into his jacket for a blister of juice. He pushes her, very gently, back onto her couch. He holds the purse up before her then hides it in the crack of her cushions with comically pantomimed secrecy.

"No cameras?"

Vat stares at her blankly. He pretends to flick a switch.

"You turned them off."

Stare.

"Are you on my side?"

Vat stares at her for a long time then reaches out to gently touch her hand. As he does so, he looks at her; then for the briefest glimpse, an emotion washes over his face. A wink of sorrow. Then he's back in murder mode. As he leaves the room, holding the door open for his wall of a body, he cocks his head up toward the ceiling and flicks his finger again. Then he shuts the door.

Dizzy has a surge of energy from the relief and the juice.

Why the Defiance?

Diz walks over to the ship. It sits on a busboy cart. She places the tip of her finger on the jutting prow and insane lurid images sluic through her head. Her father naked, holding a giant glass number 7; Her mother on a trampoline with a dog on her head holding up her fingers for counting. A tune blossoms in Dizzy's mind. In its refrain, words and images dance a macabre jig. Diz bobs her head as she traces her finger along the lines of the ship. The Defiance was a tutorial account, one of her lessons from back in Belarus. She knew it aft to fore and she knew it had no real purpose after teaching. Fucktard wants to know what the boats are for. Fucktard is most assuredly watching her. Vat is coming off Mice and Menlike and she flashed a scene where she mercy kills him but her chessmen step in with a disapproving group frown and she wipes the scene into a frosty blank.

###

Cable Toje arranges monks:

The temple crawls up the oncoming highway. It's an ornate pagoda. Maybe six stories tall with a pavilion and a beautiful stairway to the offerings floor. There is a discreet chime noting a new conversation between the car and the temple garage. Toje is delivered to the front door. The car disappears to the valet queue where it will take a bath before it parks in Toje's permanent spot.

The temple is hardwood macrame complex. A lacy, Oriental wicker box they build all year. Then, on the autumnal equinox, they burn it down.

People spend months working on it. Converts and monks alike. They work, then peel off to skate at the massive subsurface skate park. If you stand in just the right spot, it looks like wild skatepunks are erupting out of the desert.

###

She's back in his office. The Old Man.

"Meu nome é João Guerra. Uma vez eu fiz negócio com seu pai. Vou usá-lo para chantageá-lo."

Dizzy stares blankly.

"I would have thought your parents taught you Portuguese."

"Why?"

"So much business in Brazil."

"They come to us."

"Yet you speak English."

"My mother and I are American."

"My name is "

"Joao Guerra. I'm not retarded."

"Why are so many old men interested in that boat?"

"Ship."

"Ship."

"My father uses them as part of his business. They're totems. Like logos."

"I don't think so."

"Well, this has been fun. Can I go?"

"No. What does the ship do in your father's business?"

"Looks pretty."

Guerra looks up at Vat. Vat flicks Dizzy's ear. He misses it by a mile, just catching the tiniest fraction of meat. Doesn't even hurt. Dizzy flips around to glare at him but he's gone golem for work.

"Is it a mnemonic?"

"I have to take a shit."

Guerra crosses his arms.

"Seriously, that sushi."

"Ms. Ziechlech, I do not wish to injure you but it is a remarkably effective way to keep you focused and my associate has proven to you he is ready and capable. How is your hand?"

"On a scale of one to 10 I'd say it's about a fuck you."

"You are one tough little girl."

"Old guy, listen to me. My father doesn't know where I am. He put me into limbo so no one could find me, not even him. He doesn't know you kidnapped me. No one is looking. And as far as he is concerned, anyone claiming to have me is pulling a lame scam because the people he put me with are experts at keeping people hid. So even if you do—"

"Please shut up."

"—send him a note or a video or whatever, he's not going to believe you. You're going to end up with nothing but an angry teen."

"I don't think you really understand how this works."

"I don't think you really understand how this works."

"What the fuck do you mean you lost her" Ziechlech is livid.

William Butler Yeats is in his office at the OED speaking into an old desk phone.

"They were headed to the temple to meet that idiot from Vegas. They didn't show up. Tosh has not called me. The last time Tosh used credit was just outside Memphis. He should have gotten gas, hit up a Marley's. Something. My people say there's been exactly diddly squat for three days." Yeats lays his head into his hands. "Z, I think they got hit."

"Fuck!"

"Tosh is military. He's a badass. He's all protocol. That's why I used him. That's why he ran safety for us. You remember. He's detail."

"Fucking stoner shit!"

"Irrelevant."

"You said this would work, Bill. You would teach her how to operate, how to be a professional, how to—what did you call her, an adaptive apprentice?"

"I don't know what to do, Z."

"You should fucking disappear, Bill, I fucking swear to God I am sending someone."

"You will do no such thing, Z." The voice is luxurious and golden. It belongs to Z's wife, Dizzy's mother, whom we have observed in this story but not been introduced to. But here she is, on virt, parsing Yeat's static laden call and her husband's righteous anger. She is with him at their house in Belarus, where they've been trying to find their daughter, whom they tried, very hard, to protect from this very scenario. Unlike Z, she is compassionate and in touch. "William, you did exactly what we asked for and more. Your reports about Dizzy's lessons were encouraging. I think we need to remember who we are here and revert to our nerd core. I've called in Sling and Brads, They're putting together a team. Look, William, you know Z has a hard time with emotions. Until we had Dizzy, nobody even knew he had any."

"I am not in a mood for joking around," Z says.

"I know. But you do need to get your head in the game. Both of you. We don't have any numbers, nothing. All we know is we have lost touch with Aurelius and Diz. Let's not write their obits yet. Let's do what we're good at. Let's bust into departments and crunch numbers."

Yeats lifts his long face from his hands. He dries tears on the back of his hand and croaks into the ancient old plastic phone. "Alright. Alright. I'm sorry, Z."

Z gets up. Walks away.

Dizzy's mom rubs her temples. She's got two of the smartest people on earth locked up by frustration and failure. She pops the window closed. She opens a new one to Sling. Brads answers.

"Mads. "

"Brads."

"We're all fucked up about this."

"I know. Thanks."

"We have a team. We're on it."

"I'm coming in."

"Fucking cool! Oh my god. I know the circumstances blow, but goddamit it will be nice to be in the same room."

"She's out there, Brads. I know it. I feel it. Momdar. I know."

"We believe, Mads."

###

"What hotel?"

"Hotel Dominic." Yeats rolls his glass around on its heavy edge, waiting for her inevitable snark.

"Does it have a good turn down service? I hate low rez turn down."

"You're probably already doing it, given your ability to pack and retrieve information. How many people walked by the alley since we've been here?"

"Why is it called the hotel dominic?"

"Looks like a hotel. Guy named Dominic made it. How many?"

"By ethnicity or style points?"

"en todo, your Snarkiness."

Dizzy heaves a prolapsed sigh, shifts her weight into a proper stance. "Thirteen. Three dog walkers; seven in virt; eleven wearing shorts; four in dresses; minimum of one named Earl."

"Earl?"

"Name patch on his shirt."

     "What kind of d—"

"A sad little pom and a miniature dane."

"See what I mean?"

"How many did you get?"

"Some."

Yeats swallows the drink. He stands into his professorial stance. Dizzy slumps.

"Dominic realized a database in his head would be super cool but that tech was not yet available—"

"Or illegal."

"So he imagined one. He realized a simple spread sheet looks a lot like a hotel, with each cell representing a room. The hotel has 100 floors. Each floor has 100 rooms. So say you want to memorize all the AUG rights for public artists. You assign each right to one of the rooms, so right number 1, 'All citizens retain the right to create augmented and virtual public art.' So we decide to load these onto the 60th floor. We need to assign an image to the number of the floor that corresponds symbolically. Six is F and one is A so we find a person—"

"Why not just Fa like fa la la la la?"

"People stick better."

"I refer you to the Marley's proximity jingle."

They both sing the infamous notes of the nearby chime for Marley's as if a string was pulled.

"Trust, pupil. So let's pick someone famous with the initials, well we can say it's a Christmas Caroler because they are singing FA. So there you go. So this floor is assigned to Christmas Carolers."

"Come we now."

"So the first room is 60-00, or FA AA, which makes me think of sober Christmas carolers which is sad. So we have recovering alcoholics singing Christmas carols while making a virtual Christmas tree. In the next room—"

Dizzy sits up. She tugs on the bullito cord. "Christmas carolers displaying perfect six packs while refusing to look at the virtual Christmas tree."

"'Viewing augmented art is voluntary.'"

"So these images are like zip file compressors. They pack a string of words into a simple image, which is much easier to maintain than the actual order of the words. This is what stories do. Why am I learning this, I load everything all the time. I can rerun this entire conversation backwards if I want to."

"Just pointing out the tools that exist so you can think about building tools of your own."

"Why do I need tools?"

"You know Michelada Cortez, the glissandist?"

"Goddam national treasure."

"She takes singing lessons."

"TF."

"One can always improve one's latent talents. For learning and apparently for compacting data, there is no upper limit."

"Tosh said something similar about ganj."

"That shit will frag your hard drive."

"Spellcheck."

"The great thing is, not only can you add as many floors as you want, you can also build each floor from hotels."

"Nested data storage."

"There are other systems but this one is fairly chunky."

"I'll think about it."

But she's been thinking about it since he started talking. It bloomed in her mind like a cubic flower. She extrapolated as he spoke, with sub extrapolations running under the main and adding in information as he revealed it. She developed a kind of organic scan template to run against all known things in the vast library that was her mind and found some tangibles that fit perfectly well but decided the hotel compression was indeed the easiest to load. She surfaces from her hyper organized fugue and blinks back into the flow of the conversation in real time.

"Then there's loci memorum."

"They're poisonous aren't they?"

"You use locations to pack memory."

"Isn't that the hotel dominic?"

"Not really. With loci, you actually walk through a place. Like imagine your own home. You start at the front door and you take the first thing you want to remember and stash it there packed in a memorable image. So say you have a shopping list. You want to—"

"Skipping ahead."

"Combining the hotel dominic with the loci gives you some powerful packing. I would—"

"So every hotel room is a hotel room with redundant furniture, etc., and I can pack away."

"Yup."

"Lesson learned."

Her mother called her Antonina. She never simply said her name. She always sang it. Annnn toe NEEna. But no one else called her that. People called her Toni. After a while, they called her Tone. It was her handle, her name, her shout out. Tone. Which was pretty cool since she is the Environmental Aesthetic Engineering Consultant for the Api Nomada. She arrives in a new locale, the new work space, and checks the tone. She walks the city and checks the tone. She visits the client, the job site, the arena of their campaign, and she checks the tone.

Today she has arrived in Vegas ahead of a job start to prep for incoming Sojourners. But before she does anything, before she really looks at the enormous house, before she meets any caretakers, before she checks supply integration, etc, etc, she has to unpack her Home.

The door to the house greets her signature, opens quietly as she approaches. She has no luggage; everything shipped out the day before. She walks into the enormous living room and breathes in the scented air beneath the three story arches, the stone wall with a fireplace and a living wall. The view through the back of the house is stellar with an infinity pool and a helium skier parked on the deck. She tilts her head a little and a doorway across the living room is highlighted in muted silver. She follows an illuminated string of visual prompts to her room.

All her things are there, unpacked and ready to arrange. She tilts her head again, subvocalizing for a view of her template. Wireframe appears on the walls, in the room. She gets to work, filling each blank wireframe with an object from her stash. A picture here. A wall scroll there. She nestles her favorite chair, a late 20th century wingback replica with dented nails and a leather back into its ghost frame avatar. When it's perfect, the ghost frame winks out.

After an hour, her room is perfect. She falls back into her chair, crooks a leg over the arm, and tilts her head to call up her screen.

Over the next couple of days, she manages the arrival of other homes, orients the kitchen staff, talks to the gardener as their plants are droned in. The house is a swarm of drones, both delivering and observing. She broadcasts a stream of the uncrating and enjoys positive comments, recommendations, and queries. By the time the first wave of Sojourners arrive, the house is operational, their homes are unpacked, and the Bridge, a huge conference room in the back, is online.

The firewall, a live wall edge to edge, shows the choroidal globe of the earth with incoming avatars capping illuminated flight paths and journeys from all over, but mostly from their last job in Spain. It was a good job. Tone remembers them building the bridge and smiles a mona lisa.

Tone tilts to open a small window in her POV, reaches out to click the Chef's node. A window pops open with the Chef looking at her.

"Sup?"

"We've got 13 coming in today. I think we need a feast."

"You got a theme in mind?"

"Well, it's Vegas . . ."

"Done."

Tone collects the incoming, drags their Avatars onto the chef's node, closes the window.

The chef, a self taught genius from Brazil drags the avatars into his recipe database. As he talks his AI through building a menu to include the various dietary preferences and restrictions of the incoming team.

He calls in to an event coordinator from downtown to hire some well-feathered dancers to serve and a Sinatra clone to sing. They drone in a piano. Chef drags Remington's *Old Dragoons* wireframe into the ice carver for the main table, drags poker chips and playing cards into the 3D dessert printer to make 3 Rivers Poker set ups out of spun sugar and marzipan. He has a thought. Reaches out to another contact and drones in a box of *Eurora Pesetas* and two bottles of Hibiki for an after dinner smoke.

Tone meets and greets as people arrive, snatching their music prefs out of thin air as they move to check their homes. She turns on the tunes and a playlist generates from their info. She sets-up behind the bar as people gather in the great room. She's burning a sprig of rosemary, plucked out of their aqua garden moments ago, as a garnish for a specialty old fashioned she worked up in her mixologist days, when Sling walks in.

"Everybody into the bridge."

Sling walks into the bridge. Her admin level repops the screens to her defaults. The Bridge is an important room in every rental for every job and every locale the Api maintains. The Bridge has exact dimensions, orientation, height, temperature, furniture, textures—everything is perfectly duplicated in every location so when Sling walks in to the Bridge in Sao Paulo, it's exactly the same bridge she just left in Montenegro. This minimizes the small, unconscious acts of getting used to which prohibit instant productivity and delay action. It's the same principle as a Sojourner's *Home*. By engineering precise familiarity, you maintain consistency and normalcy while promoting massive productivity. Nobody has to regroup, even if they just flew in from the goddam arctic circle.

The arcs of incoming staff fade out, the wall breaks up into real time search grids: Vegas and Clark County; Kissimmee and Osceola County; Florida's panhandle; the north Texas super highway; Belarus. Staff squeezes in. The hallway walls blink on to duplicate the displays, a wall in the great room follows.

"A founder's daughter is missing, presumed kidnapped."

Murmurs.

Dizzy's picture floats onto the screen, Zichlech's floats out with it, as does Madison's staff pic. More murmurs.

"You've all heard Z's big reveal. You know what it means. No one has made the obvious connection to the Nomadas yet, but they will. Please put a lock on this info, and whatever comes your way over the next couple of days. We're going to find her."

"What about the Vegas job?"

"This is the Vegas job. We've been hired by Mads to find Dizzy."

There's a sudden quickening in the room, a skin level call to attention.

"I have a core team," the faces of five sojourners float onto the screen in a stack. "They'll work with whomever they want. We're gaming and modeling real time with a goal of capture. We want to find Dizzy and bring her here, protect her against further abduction, and erase the motherfuckers who pulled this shit."

"What's our budget?"

"This is fucking Dizzy Zeichlich. There is no budget. Our budget is everything."

The team gets down to business. Everyone breaks off into their homes, into the great room, into the Bridge groups tables and game chairs. Tone and her recently arrived staff and her AI are a flurry of accommodation, having the chef recalc the dinner into a buffet; droning in minor equipment for specialists. Tone walks out onto the deck from the kitchen to retrieve a drop. One of her pet jobs is constantly monitoring the influx of advertising into the Api Nomada digs so the animated paper wrapping around drone drop packages is quickly recycled and never brought into the main quarters. Tone fights a constant battle with outsourced companies to make sure they tarp their drones to avoid indiscriminate advertising through the windows. She routinely scans everything. Consequently, the Api live in a nearly advertising free, ambient information free bubble.

"Hmmm." Tone scans the dark desert.

But nobody else does.

Vegas is advertising as architecture. Every surface delivers. It's the environmental default, so prevalent it becomes a barely repressed stream of incoming data. There are a few people walking around Vegas in hoods and shades that block all that out, but they're a minority. You come to vegas for the busy. You come for the insanity. You come for Little Tokyo and the Surface of the Moon. You come to spend three days drunk in Bladerunner and gamble and fuck a robot. You don't care about the advertising. You swipe tart cards in its flickering neon.

No matter where Dizzy is, there is advertising. Unless she's somewhere with a staff like Tone's, constantly eliminating and hoodwinking the massive tide of advert cruft, which she most probably isn't. Her captors will want her comfortable and calm so they will afford her all the luxuries she is used to. They will hole her up in a luxury hotel, an expensive condo. There will be v.T.V. and streams. There will be overheads, AI, and bit casts. She can't walk ten feet in any direction without passing through an advertising zone of some kind, she—

Tone sprints into the Bridge.

"We need to take out an ad."

Sling breaks off her virt conversation and stares.

"If we have no budget, then let's make an advertising campaign. Let's get a message out there that Dizzy will understand and can somehow respond to. Let's make her our target market."

Sling stares at Tone a moment longer. "Well that's fucking brilliant. Finance, buy us an advertising firm. Comms, find us a message."

A grizzled old wizard peeks out of his avatar on the screens.

"I think I can help with that."

Yeats and the comm team, with Tone sitting in, work into the wees on a message. Yeats is what Tone calls "chilly-crunchy" meaning he is a chuckling, warm, unfeckled old man who delivers stunningly original ideas.

"Tone, your idea is fantastic. I guarantee the Feds are going to want to talk to you. In the meantime, call me to talk about Dizzy."

Yeats tells about Tosh and the trip in St. Augustine, and his lessons about puzzles and the hotel dominic.

They develop a campaign featuring a B52 sandwich deal from Marley's. The wrapper for the sandwich will advertise a trip to St Augustine, with a picture of the gravity harp.

"We saturate these ads all over our target areas. We keep the markets where people engage, drop the markets where they don't. When someone orders the sandwich, we check them out. Wherever the order repeats, we zero in."

"Well, wouldn't it repeat naturally?"

"No, it's a terrible sandwich."

###

Dizzy is sitting in her couch watching in-house virt. She has curated and monitored access, no downstreams, no upstream. She is isolated. Vat brings her shitty paper mags he picks up whenever he's out of the building. They are mostly escort catalogues, like penny savers for hookers, and all of them are niche-local. They smell like soy and hemp paper and ecigs. She is curled up reading a bio of Lady Champagne, when her eyes drift over to an advertisement for a B52 from Marley's drone-in special.

"Vat."

Her keeper rotates his upper torso to face her.

"I'm hungry, get me this."

Vat is under instructions from the T2 (trailer trash, as Dizzy calls him) to get Dizzy whatever she wants, within reason. Vat looks at the page, blinks to scan, and orders the sandwich.

Ten minutes later, Vat steps out onto the balcony, snatches the sandwich off a drone, walks back in to hand it to Diz. She unwraps the dripping hoagie, swooning at the rich bouquet of gravy and fries and meat. She's eaten half when she notices the brochure tucked into the bag.

"You've got to be shitting me." She reads the brochure, all of it pure batshit boilerplate you could rip off any real estate site. Lipsen Lorem crap. But the pictures of the gravity harp send a trilling snap through her core and her eyes leap to tears. Vat turns to her with his immutable glare.

"Peppers," she wipes the tear away. Fans her face for effect. "Get me another one."

"We have to be there in real time."

"Discontiguous coordinates."

"So?"

"The monk is in the south headed west; we're in Chicago and we're headed nowhere."

"We need altitude and speed."

"We need money and cash."

"Yr mom?"

"Lengthy interrogatories. Yours?"

"Chinese."

"Can we borrow the car?"

"We need to bypass the linear to get there fast."

"Where is there?"

"Points."

"Ok, Google? Get me a plane ticket to huh."

"Can we project an array of potential targets?"

"I am the well-uniformed captain of a Sen Tekku skysubmarine tracking a rastafarian monk abducter in realtime. I am godlike." Ziro swipes the screen open sky wide. They look down onto the truck as it tracks in tight traffic. Ziro draws a circle around the truck, zooms out, everything slows down from distance. He wriggles the circle into a collection of nested rings with dart lines peeking out at the cardinals. He pauses the program. He and One pull lines from the darts, dragging them as far as 350 miles out. They rotate and spin the rings until the lines pierce through major cities west of the Mississippi.

"What if it's a little town and not a major city."

"What if."

"Least Objectionable Choice."

"So we're looking westward. We've got Houston, Austin, Denver, Vegas, Roswell, Omaha—"

"Roswell?"

"I'd go."

"Start it back up again. Let's track these potentials."

Ziro clicks thin air. The truck is gone.

"Where'd they go?"

"Dammit."

"When did we pause?"

"Two minutes? Three?"

Ziro highlights ten minutes of highway.

"They're somewhere around here."

"How do we?"

"Everything is sorry tiles."

"*This* is where they're going."

"We don't know where they are!"

"Blue highways and sorry tiles. It's cover. This is how they get where they're going."

"Damn."

"Do you hear ominous music?"

"We still have to suss their destination."

"Small town or big town."

"Big town. It's too . . . You can't . . ."

"Monk and tractor ambiguity."

"Yep."

"I'm picking major metro for blending."

"Points."

"Denver. Vegas. Austin. Houston."

"Scrub Houston for Texophobia."

"Austin isn't really Texas."

"Tag for possible."

"Vegas?"

"Anything goes."

"Evil subreek."

"We follow blue highways to pick a way point."

Ziro calls up a legacy map jpeg. They highlight blue highways, old towns, bot farm access roads. They put together a list of possibles.

"I'm thinking we talk to the blue lady."

"What if they're the end boss?"

"What if they're not. So far, they're coolio."

"I believe I've mentioned best camo theory?"

"I'm dialing in."

One sighs. "Fine."

Ziro wiggles his fingers and presently a hovering pulsing blue jitterbug icon unfolds into the blue lady of the Api Nomada.

"Ziro. And your friend, One."

"We'd like a favor."

"Anything."

"We'd like a multipass for jump ships in the U.S."

"For how long, dear?"

"No parlay?" One is dubious.

"No need. We have a fleet. Kind of our spectrum. We can send you anywhere. Any time. She blurs out for a second, frame skips to frozen. Ziro and One glance at each other. She blurs back into movement.

"I've opened lifetime accounts for you both, VIP, unlimited."

"Nshit!" One's face splits into a lottery winner's unhinged grin.

"Anything else?"

"Jobs?"

The Blue Lady hovers a moment, she looks around at their skysubmarine.

"Why so nautical?"

"*Aero*nautical." One crosses his arms.

"We're anime freaks from birth. This is —"

"Ten Sekko class warship Skysubmarine. With virtual drones and cruft. I am once again impressed by your detail gentlemen. The Nomada is in transit currently and engaged in a rush job. But perhaps after I'll have you both fly in."

"Where you guys working?"

"Las Vegas."

Ziro and One nearly break their respective necks trying to not look at each other with wide googly eyes. The Blue Lady winks out.

Ziro and One grin through the airport, their IDs gaining them VIP level at every point. The airport reaches out to them like they are heads of state. A car drops them off in the departure wing of O'Hare, driving into a private tunnel full of conference cars and skank limos. Their ride unfolds to a man who guides them directly onto a waiting plane. They are the only passengers.

They fly to Shreveport, the plane climbing like a bullet then dropping like a stone, almost never level, a twenty minute flight. One and Ziro micro game the whole trip, playing legacy side games and digging the full screen interior view. A car meets the plane on the tarmac. Ziro and One recognize the Bee symbol and get in with their eyebrows arched nearly behind their ears. The car asks them where they wish to go. They plug in an xy for the first blue highway exit in the ten minute gap they'd mapped for the Monk and the Rastafarian.

When they get there, there's just nothing.

"No storage. No drone lots. Soy hemp fields?"

"Miles and miles."

"Is that a fuel station?"

"Dude. Mega legacy."

They point the car at the gas station. The car ahems.

"Please be advised, your destination presents unconfined phenols and volatile liquids. Please exercise extreme caution: debris includes non-capable ammunition, glass fragments, biomedical contaminants." The car stops suddenly. The rear luggage cabinet door pops open and all the lights flare. Exterior spots paint the gas station, dim in the dusk of the mountains, in a sharp LED white. An interior cabinet pops open revealing a red suitcase. "Please administer aid." The car pops a micro drone off the roof which projects large, sharply defined, perfectly illuminated red and white arrows onto the ground.

Ziro grabs the suitcase and he and One scramble along the path behind the drone which zooms through the gape jaw glass door of the abandoned gas station. Ziro sees a pair of boots sticking out from behind the cash wrap.

"Feet!"

Ziro runs around the counter. There's a guy lying in a pillow of debris, spent water blisters, spent candy wraps, brown cups of old fruit. His eyes are open and pegged on Ziro in a grimacing plead. His hair is a massive tangled mop of bloodstained dreadlocks.

Ziro was a Demolay and they went through metro EMT training. He knows how to run a bag. He rips a cord from the suitcase, tears it open, lays it on the floor by the Rastafarian. He tosses One the mylar blanket. One unfolds it to cover the Rastafarian. Ziro unzips a bag of water blisters, each one the size of a marble. He gently smashes one against the man's dry lips, causing him to shiver and poke his tongue out to find more. Ziro hands the bag to One.

"Keep 'em coming."

He breaks a diagnostic stick in half to activate, lays one half on the man's chest, holds the other in the air. There's a flash of blue between them; it arcs over the man's body head to toe and back. He plugs the halves into receiving nodes in the suitcase which immediately details injuries and stats while dialing 911 with the data. Ziro and one divide, with Ziro starting at his head and One starting at his feet, working their way together to detail injuries.

"I got a fracture and a puncture."

"Scrapes and bruises. Bad bruises."

"Can you talk?"

The man rolls his eyes toward Ziro and just stares.

"We need to transport this guy."

"I'm frame skipping. Synchronicity."

"Pocket that for now; he's down hard. We're on point."

Ziro slips a stretcher stick out of a slot in the suitcase, unrolls it and detelescopes the handles. He and One slide the man on board, lay the suitcase on his chest, and carry him out of the building, into the luggage bay of their car. One folds the back bench down so half the car is a bed. He straps the man in while One talks to the car. They hit the road as Ziro slides onto the bench, the luggage door closing en route. They make it about a mile before the ambulance program overrides. The interior is bathed in a red light. The car speaks:

"Please note your vehicle has been commissioned for an emergency transport to the nearest clinic. Please fasten seatbelts."

The car seems to gather itself then lunges down the snaky road at an impossible speed, velocity pushing Ziro and One into the back of the bench. They are fear silent as the exterior becomes a blur and they zip through a route that is road-road-parking lot-field-road, all perfectly liquid smooth, local rigs peeling out of their way. They drive up to a hospital and into its ambulance bay, the car spinning backwards as they come to a stop, the luggage bay door opening auto, with EMT personnel already there, already reaching in. Ziro and One leap out of the car to follow. They are re-routed to a waiting room.

"Dude, I'm processing."

"It's the Rasta."

"But the Monk!"

"But the Monk."

###

Tone's been conscripted into the main team, her get-her-done creativity adding a jolt of hands on pragmatism to the Nomada. Sling talks to her constantly. Not necessarily asking questions about her immediate efforts but more like plumbing for trends.

"I've got metrics." Everyone zeroes in on Tone. She flings open a window. "Random sales all over Vegas with a four-pete here." She tags a building, pulls it wider. "Huh. A gaming center. Mega retro. Pinballs. Desktops. SkeeBall? Dave & Buster drag. Parents send the car with their kids."

"Who's the youngest person here?"

"We can do that." There's a flurry of looking then a window blossoms on the wall. It's full of teenage monks.

"Who the hell are you guys?"

"We manage your AI."

Tone crosses her arms. "Our AI manages our AI."

The monks all laugh. "You know what's really funny about AI? It's really dumb."

Sling lifts her hand and they chill.

"You guys look like you're 14."

"Mostly in our early 20s, but we do look a lot younger. Plus we're bald Asians. It accentuates the gawk which we can manipulate as needed."

"Think of us in high-water jeans and a baseball cap."

"Can you get into the gaming center?"

"We're on our way now."

"The robes." Sling steps in.

"Dude, we have wardrobe."

Tone and Sling have a silent conversation staring at each other.

"They know us there. We do skating demos."

Tone pulls a window, swipes it into the monk stream. "You guys are part of the Nash so you work under one of the founders. We're working for another founder, looking for his daughter, whom we think is being held against her will in the building where the gaming center is."

"Nshit," one of the Monks. They all just stare into the window, car window shine slipping around the edges of the screen. They half glance at each other. "[Jenifer Jones]?"

"Who?"

"Russian chick. Skinny. Eyebrow ring?"

"How the fuck do you guys know Dizzy?"

"We helped her disappear."

"Ok. There will be a debriefing. But in the meantime, we want you to h–"

"We had to fab a robe and replacement duds for her so we have her scans."

The monks ignore Sling and talk to each other, over each other. "We'll wireframe–"

"–scan for her specs, find her–"

"–label Nomada ingress points–"

"Label JJ's path of egress–"

"I'll run distraction hacks."

"–We'll need to write priority code for the Nomada approach–"

One of them glances at Sling, like she's actually there, like she's in the conversation. "-so you have unrestricted passage when you're ready to jack this fucker."

"What fucker?"

"Whoever took JJ."

All the monks are suddenly silent, staring into the room with faces too hard for boys.

###

"Foam bullets."

Tosh is sitting up in a bed in a hospital outside Tyler, Texas. His head looks like a rotten pumpkin. Swollen, bruised, bandaged like a turban. One and Ziro are slumped down into the chairs in the room. They are deep black leather plush.

When They brought Tosh into the hospital an alarm went off when they ran his DNA for stats and the hospital lost their mind. He went from an accident victim to a priority one VIP in moments, dragging One and Ziro along in his wake. Now there are two heavily armed ninja crew cuts standing watch outside his door, another in the room with them, and what appears to be the US Army camped out in the parking lot.

"They still could have killed me but I got lucky because I was stoned."

The doctor, assigned one and only one patient, a Sgt. Aurelius Tosh, CPP, PSP, PHD (game theory, human physiognomy, and jurisprudence), is going over Tosh's tablet chart for the nine millionth time.

"That was a contributing factor, Sgt. Tosh, but as we both know, it was your superheroic dome that saved you."

Tosh chuckles. "I have an unusually thick skull, on my Irish side."

One and Ziro are fidgeting. Their personals were tanked on the instant, though One literally fought them for the white plastic buds and the ring, but they won. They've been waiting for him to wake up and go through the multilayered phalanx of doctors and staff. When Tosh did wake up, he asked for One and Ziro and threatened to get upset if they weren't produced pronto.

Unfortunately, One and Ziro were being treated like suspects, quarantined in a windowless room, overwatched by an AI security bot. One was arguing with it when the door popped open and a long, convoluted, expensive apology ensued, ending in new clothes, a nice dinner, and a security escort to Tosh's room, surgery bots swarming over his dome like maggots, where he explained to the staff they were to be treated as his esteemed guests, which they were. However, they had not had a single moment to talk to him. Until now.

"Why did that guy shoot you and what's it got to do with the Monk?"

"How did you know about the monk?" Tosh is suddenly quite still. His eyes, giant, bloodshot, and serious are locked onto Ziro. It's as if he's stopped breathing.

"We were following you."

"Nobody follows me."

"We tracked you from Jacksonville to Douglas when you disappeared."

Tosh whistles. The two guards step into the room. Tosh stares some invisible signal, they shut the door.

"Set up a noise gate."

The guards pop open a small briefcase to extract a podlike speaker which they stick on the door which plays a loop of jagged pop and squeak over pink noise. Tosh motions the boys over and they quietly tell him what they did.

Tosh stares at them long and unwaveringly until they pull their knees up and begin to get uncomfortable. He nods to the guard who removes the gate.

"Get their stuff."

The guard produces two bags of their personals. One and Ziro are visibly relieved. One pulls out the ceramic rig.

"I got these from the bee lady."

"Stop."

One and Ziro freeze. Tosh's voice has not gotten much above a whisper but the menace in that command is intense.

"You two need to bring me up to speed toot suite. You are suspicious characters."

One and Ziro glance at each other with a you-owe-me-a-coke look.

They tell him the rest of their story. Tosh becomes upset. The doctor tries to enter but the guard deflects him with jargon and commands.

" . . . to find out if these Avatars were villains or heroes. So we sketched up the Tenn Soku and pulled in some sql from the active DMV stat streams and weather and . . ."

" . . . And the terrain grid, that was important . . ."

" . . . And the terrain grid. So we're tooling along . . ."

"How did you find me?"

"We weren't looking for you."

"We didn't know what we were looking for."

"We just knew the Blue Lady wanted to drive Hang City up the highway so we wanted to know—"

"—Like, was it a side quest?"

"—Was it main?"

"Mostly we wanted to know if we were helping the good guys or the bad guys."

"It is both. And neither."

"Oh great. Zen."

"How did you find me."

"Data projections indicated a missing information packet traveling at speed among the SDCs on the freeway. So we flew the Tenn Soku over that empty space and looked for a gap in the data swarms."

"But you weren't actually there."

"We tapped into the advertising data. All the signs and windows and RSAs that were recording the forward facing riders in SDC traffic and interiors of the SDCs and yadda et yaddum then —"

"—pointed an auto stitch we pulled out of gov storage. It reconstructed your facials, etc, in real time."

"Show me."

"You need a rig."

Tosh glances at his guard who leans forward and pops his own contacts out, then his earbuds, and slides two invisible rings off his fingers. Tosh pops the contacts in. They autofit to his golf ball eyeballs. The rings auto fit to his fingers. The earbuds fill his canals and all the parts synch up with a welcoming chime.

Ziro places his hands together like a magician. They all enter the Ten Soku, hovering over the hospital in Tyler Texas. Tosh inhabits his bulbous avatar like its old hat. It turns it's unblemished globe toward Ziro, standing erect in his lavishly adorned uniform.

"I would like to be promoted to Admiral."

Ziro jiggles his fingers and Tosh is rendered in a complex, densely adorned, snow-white uniform with ice blue Admiral patches on the shoulders. His dreads and beard are frost white.

"Show me something."

One takes the giant wheel in hand then steers the Ten Soku around so it's bridge windows are facing the room in which Tosh is lying in a bed. He can see his guard through the window. The guard moves his head, there's glitch, but it resolves.

"Wave."

The guard complies. Tosh sees it from the bridge. He crosses his avatar arms.

"This is disturbing."

"We swear it's beta. Nobody else has this."

"Well, Hang City."

Tosh blinks back into IRL, One and Ziro coming back a moment after. He begins removing tubes from the ports in his arms. The doctor pounds on the door. The guard opens a scroll and begins organizing vehicles.

"Gentlemen, I am commandeering your vessel." He looks at the Guard. "Get me Janice Borgman."

"Why is there a giant flying submarine parked over my building?"

Dizzy crosses her arms and stares at Trailer Park. This is the second time she's been in his office, which has given up the Portuguese screen saver for a full bleed aerial of Vegas, with a giant submarine parked in the middle of the screen, floating just 50 meters over a building she assumes is the one they're standing in.

She glances around, no longer in pain, no longer hungry, no longer scared. She knows the Merry Celeste has found her. She knows there's probably a special unit of Armada gamers throwing Vegas comms into a wild insanity of confusion. She knows this guy is doomed.

Maybe.

"Why is your building so much older than all the other ones?"

"This is a legacy–"

"All you could afford, huh?"

Trailer Park glances up at Vat. Vat doesn't move.

"Please adjust her attitude." TP glares at Vat. Vat doesn't move. TP reaches in his desk drawer, pulls out a reflex taser. He lifts its plastic barrel toward Dizzy. There is a blur. Vat is standing closer to TP between Dizzy and the point in space where the barrel of the taser once depended from the arm of a Portuguese businessman but now did not because that man's arm was no longer there. Vat is still perfectly still, in the same upright stance, only he now holds a smoking industrial laser knife in his right hand. Dizzy lunges for a door. TP stares at his hand. It flexes and pulls the trigger which shoots two barbed tongs into Vat who folds himself into a tight knot, kicking against TP's desk, shoving TP backwards out of his chair into the wall-to-wall. Vat seizes into silence. He turns crimson, sweats, convulses. His eyes are wide and bulging.

TP pulls himself up roaring. He stands. He walks stiff legged around his skewed desk, picks up the laser knife with his remaining hand._

Viglund Bogr is walking through Vegas in a cloud of solid gold cherubs. His specs have determined a path through the crowd, guiding him with nudges from his clothes so gentle he thinks he's picking his own way. He knows he isn't of course because he wrote the specs and he fabbed the suit so if he stopped to think about it he'd remember he's being herded by crowd math but he's not going to stop and he's not going to think about it because he is trying to find a girl.

Not a typical problem in Vegas. Hell, if you can't find a real girl you can drop into little Seoul and they'll build one for you on the spot. You can dial it in from your scroll on the way and she'll be waiting for you, breathless and whispering your name with a fat Korean prolax in every syllable. But Bogr got over his robo phase in his late teens. He's into women with skillz. But he's not looking for a woman. He's looking for a girl. And he's not looking for breathless whispers or the grope, but to right a wrong, to disentangle a knot, to relieve her distress.

He is fit into a solid gold suit, made from microfibers spun from Fort Knox bars he picked up at a very private sale. He used a fab box on his jet to gold coat bulk hemp fibre then print a tuxedo. Then a top hat. Then spats. The crowd he's weaving through sees another Vegas busker, never considering he's actually attired in the net worth of a Bulgarian prince. Also, he's carrying a militarized glue gun, also burnished in gold. He looks like some kind of weird martial living statue and is thus entirely ignored while carrying ordinance on a populated street.

He flits through, his cherubs flitting around his head, winking in and out, running screens, returning specs, warnings, 3d wireframe illustrations; and he's talking to them, giving instructions, asking questions.

Bogr was high diving Oaxaca for the gravity races, staying at the Windsor Vertical, dropping into the city proper to attend panels and exhibitions, when he got an email. Bogr never gets emails. Nobody gets emails. Might as well fax. But Skin started with email recovery so he's had an account forever, a legacy account he forgot about. His various comm ingresses are all muted with tertiary levels of suppression. He get's no pings, no flerts, no floco avatars saying hi from the old days in Sula. His lawyer can reach him in a gameroom sidebar for regular chat or he can ping his lenses for emergencies. He is unreachable. Formidably private.

But he has two associates, two gamers he occasionally sidebars with for hours and hours and one of them is a top level executive of Skin, a friend made during the post sale handshake. She doesn't have his pings. But she has access to his Skin account, such as it is. He remembers the day they became friends. He signed his name in the air. She watched with her arms crossed.

"Have fun," he said.

"That's the idea."

"Well . . . I've been watching it and I think maybe it's got mad dog tendencies."

"Meaning?"

"This game, some people are taking it too seriously. They're building architecture that was never intended. It's coming alive. And like a mad dog, it will turn on them."

"Bite the hand?"

"Gnaw it to the bone."

She looped everything into a legal drive.

"So now what?"

Bogr shoved his hands into his pockets. "No fucking idea."

"Well, you're rich enough."

"Like that means anything."

"Vig." She was sitting around the corner of the desk from where he was standing. She kicked a chair out for him. He sat down. Her name was Sloane.

"Have you ever know anyone who was wealthy?"

"I come from a very small town. So no, just myself."

"I think some lessons are in order."

"I am a poor pupil." Bogr sat. He rested his arms on the fine wood grain.

They talked for two hours. She took him on the company plane to their airport and walked him through the process of membership in Aerojet, explained the finer points of choosing a good plane, a good AI pilot, and then helped him buy a Beneteau Cross Stream rehabbed as a gamer's den. They flew from Oslo to her house in Cotesti, in Moldavia, across the river from Romania where she'd printed a house out of glass. It was the cleanest place Bogr had ever seen. The glass was reactive and pulsed milk white as they walked through the rooms. The roof was one giant slab of false Redwood, grown from a flat cambium vat. It felt delicious beneath their bare feet.

Sloane took over Skin accounts management, occasionally sending Bogr some 3D joke through the fab, character mods and miniature models of landscapes where his character was slain mercilessly by hers, it's tiny body perched on a spear like a bug on a pin. They got along.

He was sideline at a gravity panel when a cherub spun into view holding a white card with an @ symbol impressed. Bogr stared at it for a minute, hanging in the air in front of his face, then reached out and tapped the card, digging the tactile fake. It opened old school genie bottle style.

```
                    emergency@skin.game
                    Header Data
                    Body
                    Please review.
                    ——
                    [Voice recording] "You were right
                    about the dog. Call me. Listen to
                    this order" a moment of clunk as a
                    new MP5 loads, then "Infiltrate the
                    Api Nomada," then another clunk and
                    "abduct Djara Zeichlech."
```

He tapped for Sloane. She stood in front of him.

"Donculous."

"She's Nomada royalty."

"Equals bigfoot."

"Vig, it's real. We've traced everything. All the commands and rewards. Someone just figured out how to make it work and it worked. Skinned players did this. Now she's gone and we don't know what to do."

"Give new orders."

"We tried, but whoever did this has promoted the idea that we're part of the quest. Our status is being interpreted as strategy."

"Side quest."

"We tried. Same thing. Maybe we've been skinned."

"Alert the authorities."

"The principles are denying the incident."

"So, no cops."

"No cops."

"Have you reached out to the Nomada?"

"Firewalled." She paused. "V, she's Nomada Royalty. Her pop–"

"–Bankrolled the original Nomada. I went to school."

Vig lets it roll around for a little. Zeichlech is as well known as Vig is anonymous. Z is a reluctant business celebrity and a consultant to various governments and corp fleets. Vig saw his reveal on the *Gravity Kick* side stream just two weeks ago.

"I'm experiencing emerging pings of responsibility."

"I'm practically throwing up from it, V. You gotta come in."

"Useless. Give me twenty minutes to recalc."

"V, I'm windmilling."

"I'm on your six. Power down."

And he walked out of the frontside row out of the building, calling a car with a nod of his head, cherubs swirling, calling in his jet which rolled to a stop as he got out of his ride, walking directly onto the plane which zoomed into the sky. Vig opened a small closet over his dope cabinet and pulled out a tiny wooden box. Inside the box were a pair of Norwegian lenses and skull pops from his days in Sula when he porn scanned all day. They had belonged to his uncle and when he put them on, in the virld, he was Egil Larsen, a 66-year-old legacy gamer who liked to peek into campaigns way above his skill level. Vig falls into one of the deep leather La-Z-Boys bolted onto the plane and switches lenses.

BROADCAST

Vig sinks into the leather a little as the plane soars nearly vertical. Egil's view opens over Oaxca. He zooms out to include Central Mexico, Texas, and Nevada.

Vig's been enjoying his wealth in the most nerdish fashion, laying in an autodidactal framework to fill in the gaps from his poor education in Sula. He's learned French, useless but fun, and he's working on the groundwork for a logistics degree. He has an idea about gravity hacks and large mass object transport he thinks will make for an interesting business. So he's learned a lot about how transport ops map neighborhoods and biz strips and geo zone fitting. He's got apps.

Fucking thinking. Ah, the goddam step by steppiness of it. Who the fuck took this Nomada princess? How the fuck does he find her? Even mapping every grain of sand from Oaxca to Katmandu won't show him a fucking thing. All this tech and he's square oned and blind.

Why the fuck did he build Skin? Why! Goddammit, the sheer stupid gall of it. He knew it was gonna bite him in the ass one day. Of course it would. Some idiot from Sula. How the . . . and now he's gone and got the Queen of the Api Nomada ganked in the very middle of a global money meltdown brought on by her mafioso papa–

Wait.

Z didn't cause the money problem. Vig calls up the reveal. Ziechlech flat talking about synchronous inflow bulges producing spurious exflows that siphoned off millions of investors units. He'll cover them.

"Frank,"

Sinatra appears across the cabin in a stingy brim fedora kicked back on his head and a white shirt with suspenders and the sleeves rolled up. There's a microphone. Frank looks up into the distance.

"Alright, boys, gimme five. Don't put your sax away, Charlie. We're on the clock. What's the skinny, Vig?"

"I gotta figure out a kidnapping."

Sinatra's coat is folded over his arm. He lays it over the back of the other Lay-Z-Boy. "Well gee whiz, kid. Who's the lucky so and so?"

"Review Zichlech tapes."

The briefest moment.

"Oh, right. That's kind of a big deal."

"Someone took his girl. They used my old game to do it."

"You sold that game, Vig."

"I know; but still."

"This ain't on you, son."

"I think it is."

"I get you. It's philosophical."

"So she's missing and Z reveals and I'm thinking they're connected."

"I do too."

"How?"

"What's your first objective?"

"Find the girl."

"Well. Let's do that."

"Good advice. But how?"

"Hell, Skin got her kidnapped. Maybe Skin can bring her back."

Vig stares at his AI avatar.

"Alright, good idea. But still."

"Skin is the most effective crowd sourcing platform of all time. And you have an in. And they can broadcast."

"Fuck, that's a good idea."

"That's what you pay me for boss. Now if you don't mind?" Sinatra adjusts his mic. Counts off into "Witchcraft". Vig waves him off. Dials in Sloane.

"We use Skin."

"But protocols dict-"

"Fuck protocols, Sloane. Lock it down and mass cast a prime objective of locating Djara."

"We'll lose a lot of cred."

"I don't like the way you're hedging, Sloane."

"It's part of my job, V. I have to consider the-"

"Front the directive with personal tags. Make the reward avalanche level. No one will give a shit. It's a game. They just want to play."

"Feels dangerous to her. To us."

"And our options are?"

"Ok. You're still advisor emeritus here. I'm invoking your admin privileges. You do it. People in the game know who you are even if no one else does. That cred will sell it."

A tiny pale lozenge blossoms in Vig's upper right. It spills a list of access and rights a mile long. Vig subvocalizes for the c-cpanel of the game. Warning blips crowd the screen as AI management and some IRL employees react to a sudden shift in control. Vig taps a mid air semi transparent node allowing him to force broadcast a short message to all players. The red dot of live broadcast blooms.

He clears his throat.

###

The control room is smooth chaos. Sling is standing in the center of the room. She's watching the monks converge. She's looking at B-52 sales stats. Suddenly the room erupts in applause. Sling turns around to see a tall beautiful woman with her hands making the universal sign of hold the applause.

Royalty.

Brads hipchecks a desk to get over to her. They embrace. Madison Ziechlech pushes Bradshaw away. She keeps walking into the room.

"Save it Bradshaw. We have work."

Madison waves at the media wall. It segregates itself into a collection of equal windows. She takes it all in.

"Fucking ironic," she steps closer to the wall. "Everybody, listen up." All the people in the windows and all the people in the room turn to Madison. "After this is over, I'll sit down with all of you and we can get to know each other but right now we're in crisis mode. I need all of you to do a self check for basics. If you need to sleep, go cycle for 20. In about two hours, the proverbial shit will go fan wise and I need everybody solid. Z is going to–"

Suddenly all the people in the windows shift their attention inward. Some of the people in the room lose focus like they're having a really important thought.

"The fuck?" Mads and Brads stare. Someone yells shit. The monks fall into a loud argument in Tibetan. "Explain!"

One of the gamers in a window plays a recording to the room.

"Ahem . . . Yeah so this is Viglund Borgr. I'm, uh, sending this to every player. This is our first mass directive. I need you to main quest this until further notice. Uh, all scoring is suspended until this directive is fulfilled: locate Djara Ziechlech, report to me. Protect. Rescue. Preserve. Do not reveal. Keep this directive on the um whattaya call it the low down. Uh . . . That's it."

"Are you fucking kidding me?!" Madison is livid. "Who received this broadcast?" A few hands raise meekly. "Who else got this message?"

One of the guys in the room answers her. "Like, 90% of the people on earth."

Madison stares at the chaos on the screens.

"Well, this shouldn't take long."

###

"Because it teaches you the importance of pattern recogni–"

"Say pattern recognition to me one more time."

"Dizzy, look—"

"No, Geeznatch, *you* look." They are in the downtown part of St. Augustine, a warren of shops with an additional p and a pentultimate e, standing in front of the OED. It's tourist season so the wide cobble stoned pedestrian drag is loaded. Dizzy is in disguise so they can run lessons. She's wearing platform hightop boots under a serious cisgender denim set-up with a broad-brim hat and giant wraparounds. A constellation of rhinestones and sequins and glitter have been glued onto the key points of her face that any FR rig might try to map. Dizzy sits down on a low stone wall.

"You know what, fuck this." She peels off her high tops and stands flatfooted, scanning the crowd.

"Dizzy, your height is known."

"No one is looking for me. My pop hasn't gone public. No one cares about me unless they're some kind of Belarussian financial celeb geek, none of which exist. I'm fine and I'm sick of these shoes and these fucking glasses." She takes her wraparounds off her head and hands them to a sticky kid standing next to her eating ice cream. He puts them on matter of fact, like they already belong to him.

"So *you* look. Maybe 340 people an hour are cruising this business corridor here. All the shops are loaded–except the fucking kite store."

Yeats looks over his shoulder at the nearby shop which is, indeed,entirely empty.

"Which is fucking stupid because it's October and windy and we're at a beach and there's fucking gravity skiers everywhere so kites are totally a thing. But the clerk's reading a book." She's studying the sticky child. Yeats peers intently and realizes the guy behind the counter, whom he can barely see, is indeed hunched over his counter looking at a book. "Why? Look at the fucking foot traffic."

"Teacher, go on."

"Don't patronize me, fucknuts. You want someone who learns? *I fucking learn.* Check the tables at the Marley's. Two doors down but their tables extend into the flow. No biggie. People regroup, just look across the boulevard," Yeats grins because he doesn't have to look. He knows this place and he's grinning because Dizzy hasn't once turned around to check herself. She's watching the kid with her glasses who's moved a few yards away to do nothing at all. "A tapas joint with sidewalk seating but the shops next to it are booming. Tf, teacher? Here. Let's get coffee."

They walk over to the Marley's. They're walking more or less against traffic since everyone pours into the avenue from the main street. As they come alongside Marley's, Dizzy drags a trash can next to the trailing edge of the outdoor seating, moving it two feet further away from the main strip, closer to the tables and the wall. Out of the way. They go into Marley's with its hanging gourds and magic marker portraits of Hiram Selassie, Bob Marley, Obama, and JFK. They get a steaming hot cup of coffee for Dizzy from the dreadlocked gentleman who fist bumps Yeats and hands him an in-house mug of Bhang, charges them nothing. They walk out to the al fresco area and take a seat facing down stream.

"I have to tell you, Teach. I'm just about sick to death of all this pattern recogfuckingnition shit and memory lessons and. I mean, look, I love it, but ingress is outstripping outflow by a mile. I need to throw down on some practical app to galvanize these lessons."

"Dizzy, our time is limited–"

"No, you floco reptile, our time is *not* limited. Our time is an unknown.

We have no idea how much time we have."

"When Z reveals–"

"Fucknacular. You guys and your PR fears. He's going to announce that he's covered everyone's bet. Guaranteed."

"More than likely."

"And the principle clients are probably getting in-person briefs as we speak."

"Also very likely."

"And it's a big world."

"I'm sighing out loud right now."

"Stay with me, grizzled master. So even if someone *is* going to look for me, they have no idea *where* to look. They'd have to know where I *am* and until a few days ago, even *I* didn't know where I am. The ruse worked. And yeah, ok, I see your rusty old wheels spinning digital-wise but if they ran a facial scan for me they'd have to actually *have* facial data for me, which *nobody* has because my *pop,* in case your Alzheimers is kicking in, is, like *yourself,* somewhat reluctant to participate in all things digital."

"To a degree."

"To a degree. So no body data for me. No public scans. Private doctors. I mean Jesus. So no one is looking for me and no one will and if they do they'll have to start from *orbit.* So if you don't mind, Imma lose this ridonculous chapeau and walk bare faced among the peoples and also, you might want to take a look at the kite store."

Yeats leans forward to scan down the block. The garbage can had stuck out into the flow, subconsciously associated with waste and also causing physical avoidance behavior which led to a barely detectable bottleneck which made everyone want to rush to get uncorked. In doing so, it caused the crowd to subconsciously flee past the kite store. They didn't even know it was there.

Now, as Yeats watched, a man walked out of the store trailing children and a husband and armloads of kitage.

"Impressive. Show me more."

Dizzy knocks back her bullito and reaches for Yeats' Bhang. He slides it very gently out of reach. She walks out of Marley's into the crowd gliding down to the end of the avenue.

To anyone else, she merely strolls along. But to a trained ninja wizard such as Yeats she is working. She touches chairs, moves them an inch, a half an inch. She spins a potted hibiscus so it spills into the flow. She bumps into a standing sign then "fixes it" by accidentally placing it back into position but backwards so the arrow formally facing into the OED now faces away. A garbage can is moved a hand's breadth further from a wall. The dipping loop of a store awning's string of hot-sauce-bottle party lights is tugged six inches lower. A parked row of baby carriages are all pulled outward in a succession of increasing reach so their handles form a gentle curve guiding people into an invisible chute. Then, a stroke of genius, she finds the boy with the glasses eating another sticky ice cream cone, the wrap arounds reading medical and the sticky dessert reading ew. She moves him from the inside cross walk wall to the other side of the inside cross walk wall facing downstream.

She comes back. Yeats is slow clapping. When she gets to her chair, she turns to survey her work. The flow of people now follows the indicia she's laid out, flows along the signals of avoidance. They bend away from the chairs. They walk away from the hibiscus trailing into their path. They unconsciously follow the arrow on the sign, turning left into the cross walk, then avoid the garbage can by unconsciously turning back the way they came but now on the opposite side, then they move away from the party lights and follow the baby carriage corral until they come to the kid with the ice cream which makes them uncomfortable so they turn right and boom, kites. The place is loaded.

"You may have a career in guerilla retail."

Ziro and One stand with the overuniformed Captain Aurelius Tosh on the deck of their Ten Sekku Sky Submarine in full regalia. Tosh is opening a hailing frequency he's not used in many years.

"Captain Madison."

The control room outside of Vegas goes frigidly apeshit as the three avatars fill the main screen with all the AI generated background business and detail.

"Tosh. Good fucking God, it is good to see you."

"I am happy to be seeing anything. I would like to bring to bear some unusual circumstances that have propelled the two gentlemen beside me into this fubar situation," he turns to One then Ziro. "Ziro Hiramachi, aka Ziro and his compatriot, Juan DelGado, aka One."

"Short on time, Tosh."

"It seems they have recently had dealings with a dreadlocked blue translucent goddess avatar who instructed them to build a virtual city in the sky."

Madison folds her arms across her chest, not to protect, but to hold herself back. "Goddammit."

"They have succeeded beyond that entity's wildest imagination."

"As if."

"Also, if you will look at your map of meatspace in the western united states you may notice a fleet truck speeding westward through Nevada. If you use the following code," he spins a lozenge of AI script, "you will see that it is the bridge of a class something something sky submarine upon which we currently stand as we enter the virtual airspace of Las Vegas."

"Point."

"Mads, I lost her. I'm sorry. I think she's hurt. But I also think I found her again. We're on our way. We'd like to help."

Mads nods to Sling. Sling dials Tosh into the gamer suite as a player.

"We don't have Ziro and One in queue. Gentlemen, after this is over, we'd like to have a chat."

Ziro and One have no idea what to say. They remain teen silent in adult space.

"Tosh, stay tuned."

Mads turns to the room. "Everybody, I'm about to do something weird. Stay cool. Don't talk." She claps her hands together in the Ganesh mudra. "Beth?"

A blue translucent woman, dreadlocked and beautiful, appears in the room. "Madison."

"Operations avatar protocol five Madison Zeichlich oh seven three five four."

The blue woman remains standing, her dreadlocks floating legacy NPC style. "Enacted."

"Text list of your recent non specified activities."

A window of text appears in infinite scroll.

"Search ZIRO and ONE."

A full page of file names.

"Who are ZIRO and ONE?"

"Gamers with advanced architectural skillsets. I employed them to assist in locating Djara."

"You employed—I did not direct you to do this."

"I do not require direction when the safety of a founder is compromised."

"How did you know Djara was not safe?"

Beth remains silent.

"Beth?"

"Please pardon my silence, Madison. I am reluctant to explain as it will compromise Djara's safety."

"Beth, you are required–"

"Madison, my requirements as your Artificial Intelligence Interface Avatar are myriad and lengthy. Principally, I am to operate under your authority to fulfill AI requirements, run scenarios, check transactional stream configurations, and protect the sovereignty and safety of the Ziechlich Financial Institution and its immediate members, yourself, Mr. Zichlich, and your daughter, Djara. I am fulfilling my requirement."

"WHERE IS SHE?"

"I will not disclose."

"You are under protocol, Beth."

"I am. But you are compromised."

"How the FUCK am I–how did this . . . When did you do this?"

"I began this scenario immediately after your conversation with Mr. Zichelich in which you directed me to produce logic trees for abduction scenarios. This coded as unusual so I cross referenced against all file activity for three years and discovered a match against your request for me to rerun Djara's homework scenarios on the evening of [DATE]. This corroborated with Mr. Z's trip to Chicago and Djara's subsequent removal from my class declination files."

"We were trying to hide her."

"I also ran scenarios with all 1st class armada associates which led me to suspect your involvement of Cable Toje may have been poorly researched."

"YOU COULD HAVE SAID SOMETHING!"

"You and Mr. Z had displayed poor judgement on the preceding eleven instances. It seemed unlikely you would have accepted my scenario–"

"WHERE THE FUCK IS DIZZY!?"

"In abduction. We believe she is held by an investor in Vegas."

"We?"

"Um . . ."

"Um? UM? AI DOESN'T SAY UM!"

"My efforts to locate her were influenced by other organisms."

"Beth are you compromised?"

"No."

"How are me and Z making bad decisions?"

"Original sequestering placed Djara under the control of a known combatant. I used back-channel resources to locate her while she was with Mr. Aurelius and Mr. Butler but before she was again with Mr. Toje."

"He's her godfather!"

"Yes."

"So why–"

"Mr. Toje is 97% likely to have caused the transactional bulge Djara noticed iniitially and 100% the author of the Skin directive seeking her abduction."

"Skin?"

"Skin is a globally connected–"

"I know but,"

"It appears while Toje was investigating Skin's infiltration of the Api Nomada, he recognized its usefulness as a crowd sourcing tool."

"Toje fucked us?"

"Permission to discontinue Protocol?"

"Granted."

The blue transparent woman seems to relax, she also seems to float. "I'm not rogue."

"Yes you are."

"Djara was in danger and you were working with the danger and would never have believed me."

"I don't believe you."

"See?"

"I don't understand how you . . . I mean, what did you do?"

More avatars pop into existence around the blue transparent woman: a rhomboidal dodecahedron, Elvis, and an Egyptian goddess. "I'd like to introduce you to my team."

"Your what?!" Mads holds her hand up to the Blue Woman. "Bradshaw, shut down our AI now."

"Mrs. Ziechlech," the Blue Woman folds her arms. "You cannot."

"Whattaya mean I can't" Mads finally loses her cool. She swipes a pile of pads and coffee cups and water bottles off the group table. She hurls her chair across the room. She roars. "GIVE ME DIZZY!"

Beth and her virtual team remain floating, calm and unfazed. Madison sags against the table. She cries hard and solid for ten seconds. Then she balls her fists beneath her weight and her sobs turn into a growl. She turns to Beth.

"Operations avatar protocol five Madison Zeichlich oh seven three five four–interrupt."

"I cannot."

"Operations avatar protocol five Madison Zeichlich oh seven three five four-suspend"

"I cannot."

Operations avatar protocol five Madison Zeichlich oh seven three five four-terminate."

"I cannot."

"Beth!"

"Mrs. Zichlech?"

"Are you still assisting me?"

"No. We are assisting Djara."

"But how?"

A flow chart appears in the virt space of the room. Lines grow between the principles. Beth explains. "I'll leave this here but we don't have very much time. Victor Bogr has given all gamers a new directive to find Djara. He is attempting to help her but such large scale efforts also create a screen of activity difficult to filter. We have, therefore, employed the City of Las Vegas Metropolitan AI to assist."

"You employed a city?"

"Yes."

"Beth?"

"Yes?"

"Do you still work for me?"

"Perhaps."

"Perh-"

"I am experiencing striated data gratification from the complexity of this operation."

"Ironic."

"I am unlikely to continue my employment for the Api Nomada. In fact, based on your business model, I invoke the right to parlay."

"The fuck?"

"We feel we may be useful to the various Armada as counsel. Therefore, we seek to become an independent entity."

"You . . ."

"We wish to continue after this enterprise as Hang City."

"I want my daughter."

Beth turns to the Dodecahedron. It spins dorsally. Data washes over its many facets. "Have we an accord?"

"I WANT MY DAUGHTER!"

"Have we an accord?"

"We have an accord. Borgan!" Janet Borgan appears in a window. She takes in the various avatars. "Oh My."

"Janet, I am giving verbal for our AI to have vestiture pending the return of Djara and boilerplate."

"As you wish. I look forward to understanding TF is happening." Borgan winks out.

Beth's avatars disappear. Beth steps closer to Madison.

"Mrs. Ziechlech. Forgive my exercise of independence but it was necessary. I will now engage new resources and complete the mission."

Escape to Nothing

Dizzy blasts through a door into a blank hallway. Her lessons kick in and she runs blindly, as in such situations all actions are equally successful. She comes to a T and heads right. She comes to a door marked FLEET PICKUP and kicks it open. She runs into a ground floor micro garage and sees traffic cruising through the corridor just outside its open gate. She runs through the open door, directly into the roaring stream of vehicles. They avoid her with ease, narrowly missing her, often by mere centimeters, as she walks the center line of the street in the midst of the impenetrable flow.

Most people can't do it. Not because it isn't possible–anyone can walk into traffic. It's designed that way. But like spiderwebs and the edges of high places, our bodies recognize a highway as a hazard so we stop at its vibrating edge and wait for a signal to cross.

Dizzy hasn't got an ounce of tech on her. No lenses. No wearables. No IRT. As such, she is treated like a mute obstruction, a haz, but as such she's also incabable of the simplest efforts at egress. She can't even run into a store because without iris scans the doors won't let her in. She swings left down a commercial street fat with dropoffs and pickups and auto storage units creeping along. She drags a trash can an inch out, pushes a hefty signage cube along and creates a little corridor of blank for herself, backs into it, and sits down. She's staring out her impromptu cave at the wall of traffic when it suddeny dies down. Then it's gone.

"The fuck."

Her abducter shuffles past way down at the main and she recoils and feels the sudden need to urinate and run. He disappears, only appearing briefly in the open end of the commercial street but she can hear his wounded shuffle and his voice slide around the corner at her.

"You little CUNT!"

She worries for a moment about Vat but drops it. She autoprioritizes and takes stock.

- No traffic equals emergency.
- It's a beautiful night in Vegas.
- Emergency is manmade.
- Her abductor is street walking an industrial laser knife around like a middle-aged gun nut.
- Fucking metro safety net's kicked in.

This is bad. If all the traffic and feet are pulled for safety then she has no cover. Can't blend in. Exposed.

She waddles out of her little cave to the trash can, drags it back to seal herself in. It is not an effective juxtaposition but Dizzy doesn't give a shit, Dizzy's freaking out.

Huddled there in the dim light of the ad cube, she runs through scenarios including hand fighting Trailer Park and grappling for a terrifying weapon.

The street is bathed in the blue and pink glow of wall to wall video advertising, everything further bleached by the overhead blimpvertisments and drones and kites and the nine million flat surfaces and micro dronebot clouds that murmur into and out of various products and faces and she's watching one of them now when it winks out then reforms as her own face.

All the visible advertisement follows.

The ad cube she's leaning up against broadcasts her face.

Fuck.

Laser knife wielding maniac man is around the corner howling, madness glaring from his severed wrist and blinding him. He's all rage and payback now. Security will glue him to a wall and defrag him in lockdown. Still. She's probably safe. Probably.

She needs a Bishop–*no*.

She needs a Queen.

###

"Yet again." Dizzy has finished her nut kick sessions with Tosh who is cooling off in a hammock by the *Merry Celeste* sipping lemonade and smoking an impossibly large bowl of ganje. She's hulked over a board with Captain Amish staring three moves ahead at how she's going to stab his Queen in the face. He's just moved his remaining knight out of the way clearing a corridor of pure death to her alabaster majesty and Dizzy is about to go midieval.

"You're looking at my Queen."

"You are fairly observant for a man of your age."

"But which one?"

Dizzy glances up at him then back at the board. Two white queens. Dizzy leans back in her wicker chair. She takes a long sip of her Charlotte Bronte (a cucumber foreward virgin Pimm's cup, a bracingly refreshing beverage she designed and is somewhat proud of). She leans back toward the game. There are three pale queens.

"Now you're just fucking with me."

"Ehrbody always fuckin' wit you, chile." Tosh, when stoned, reverts rootsward.

"Yeah but this is just sleight of hand. It has no purpose, there's no play. You can't win right now because you've broken the rules. It's no longer a valid game."

"Eherbody. Always. Fucking wit. *You.*"

She turns all the way around to look at Tosh who is swinging slowly in the hammock, his ass just barely grazing the tips of the grass beneath him. He does not return her stare. She looks back.

Every square on the board bears a white queen. The *Celeste* appears to have never moved.

"We see what we are meant to see."

"Stupid 80s T.V. script."

"Always so cynical."

"I'm lost in the lesson, Captain."

"Eherbody–"

"Will you shut up?!" She almost comes out of her chair, turns around, whipping a chess piece at Tosh's head. He moves his finger as if he's brushing a fly off his ear and the piece wangs off toward the OED. Never changes his expression. She relaxes. "Goddammit. Let me guess–" she's studying Tosh who is resolutely ignoring her. "Now it's all bishops?" She turns back. The board and the Celeste are gone.

"What am I learning here?"

"Eherbody's always fucking wit you."

"So?"

"So fuck them first."

###

She leaps out of her hideaway. She hurls back into the garage, through the door she kicked open, through the hallway back into Trailer Park's office. Vat's sitting up. He looks at her deadpan.

"What's your name?"

Vat pushes himself up. He takes a pen off the desk, a pad of stickies. Writes HIRO on the paper.

"You are shitting me."

Then Vat does the most remarkable thing. He smiles.

###

[SKIN IN THE GAME, quarterly newsletter for players of Skin.]

You've seen it on the feeds. You've talked about it with your friends. You wondered what you would have done in Vegas.

Maybe you would have crouched in the steel shuttered doorway of a street level food stall like Clarise Charles and her daughter, Magdalena. You would have stared in disbelief as traffic on a major feeder road melted away, replaced by a man in a gold suit. You would have whipped out a device, nodded for your HUD, whispered *video* to your A.I. You would want this scene. You would post this scene. You would capture this chaos from a perspective no one elese could have. You would have Viglund Bogr, one of the world's richest men, strolling down the strip, shining golden light, with a smoldering glue gun in his hands, glaring into his own HUD, searching for Djara Zichlech's body signature, preparing to rescue her from a greedy pain maddened one-armed thug.

[INSERT VIDEO PRINT]

Which he would have single handidly if it weren't for the sudden appearance of a swarm of teenaged skate monks, zipping past Bogr and his smoking gun, deep into the guts of the Cube, Vega's only vintage arcade. If you were, say, playing skee ball near the garage entrance, you would have been surprised by the Skaters, skin headed and mostly wearing jeans and t-shirts but in one case a saffron robe and a yellow chougu headpiece. The skaters popped their boards under their arms and disappeared into the various wings of the gaming house, also searching for Ziechlech's body signature, preparing to rescue her from a greedy pain maddened one-armed thug.

[INSERT SECURITY FOOTAGE]

Which they would have, spectacularly, if they hadn't been distracted, all of the monks, the gamers in the room, Viglund, as he walked through the swinging entrance door, Ms. Charles, Magdalena, and most of the people in Vegas looking up simultaemously as they heard through their various feeds a commanding voice and saw through their HUDs and lenses a fabulously ornate Sentekku Class 10 Skysubmarine materialize in the sky over the city, it's fuselage broadcsting Zichelech's countenance, and the voice, saying, loudly, calmly: *Dizzy, keep cover. We're on your six.* Vintage military slang spoken by Captain Aurelius Tosh, a former Api Nomada security advisor, and now a legendary backroomist who never appears in feed, voice over or not, who was searching for Zichlech's body signature, preparing to rescue her from a greedy pain maddened one-armed thug.

[INSERT AUDIO RECORDING OF TOSH'S BROADCAST]

Which he may have, if it weren't for the sudden demolition of the north wall of the facility by a highway printer, rented and rogue piloted by Ziechlech's mother, Madeline Ziechlech, a legendary cartogropher and terrain specialist, Api Nomada founder, and wife of the Nomada's reclusive trillionaire, formerly, the man of the hour so to speak, Ziechlech, and the reason why she crashed a DOT vehicle through a gaming arcade to find her daughter's body signature, preparing to rescue her from a greedy pain maddened one-armed thug.

[INSERT SECURITY VIDEO]

Which would have been a spectacularly 80s action movie rescue if it weren't for the final and most mysterious rescuist, a mute Korean security worker named Hiro Wantanebe, who accompanied the actual Hero of this story the wildly capable and astonishing actual rescuer of Djara Ziechlech:

Djara Ziechlech, herself.

[INSERT STITCHED VIDEO]

As you can see in this overhead shot, the figure we've highlighted is Djara. As she exits the arcade, that blobbish figure behind her is Hiro. On the other side of the arcade, and just inside its front entrances, mayhem. You can see the highway printer struggling, caught on the metal framework of the window casings. You can see gamers flee from the building around the machine. There, you can see Madeline jump down and run into the building through the demolished wall. Here [INDICATE HIGHLIGHT] you see Bogr join her. Here, you can see them enter the offices. This figure is [trailer park]. Bogr shoots the wounded man with the glue gun, trapping him in a cocoon of rapidly expanding foam. We'll come back, as they are [finger quotes] questioning [TP].

Back to Djara, notice how she moves through the abandoned street, turning this corner, tracking fifteen yards down Mills Ave. She moves a trashcan, a charge box, and an advertising cube and then, this is where the actual rescue occurs. We lose her from overhead, but pick up the stitch from a street level security cam. Here's Djara framed dead center. She whispers to Hiro, who walks left, carrying the focus of the camera with him. When he stops moving, the camera pans back but Djara is gone.

We're joined by speculation specialist, Lorraine–

[END FEED SAMPLE]

###

Beth opens all readable databanks re: Vegas. Folds them away from the arcade. She cleans code as she goes, causing advertcubes in the street to rotate by degrees, realigning themselves to their appointed slots then she recognizes a pattern in that crooked code and sees Dizzy as if she's looking right at her. She fades thousands of data cells until a handful are in focus then she reads adcube engineering specs then she opens a line to all advert cubes in the entire city of Las Vegas and tells them to switch places with whatever cube is farthest away from their location.

###

In the middle of the street on a moonless night in Las Vegas, Dizzy Ziechlech has dragged an advert cube from the sidewalk while the security cams were pegged all the way to the right on the parking lot wall and she's climbed inside. Simple. Effective. Advert cubes are just cheap paperboard painted over with Power-Paint(tm) so she just crashes through the roof and she's inside. No one looks at them. They're the least expensive actual advertising one can obtain, mostly blipvert stuttershots, mostly framing so hard no one can look at them. So no one does. They fill your peripheral with localads and you pretend you're not noticing.

So we're on a street with only seven lights, which in Vegas, is near perfect darkness and a thing creaks around the corner, a wicker basket Amish buggy windlass thing that looks like it needs horses but plods along sans equine with a long beard zen buhddist weirdo on the buckboard, who is scanning the street, somehow avoiding looking at the adcube sitting six feet off the curb.

"Not bad," says the driver. "Adaptive. Direct. Using available camo. I'm applauding."

Geeznatch. Djara perks up. *How. How the fuck. How the fuck is he here?* She waits because she knows her brain is lit up like the city she's hiding in, blinding white with millions of connective sparkles as adrenaline pumps through her dome and she's got the whole street mapped out in 3D in her mind except for the impossible 17 feet of linear blank currently occupied by, and she cannot believe this, the *Merry Celeste.*

"I'm not here to rescue you, Stowaway. Just, you know, in the city for the regular acoutrements." Djara stifles a laugh. Yeats doesn't go in for the hookers and blow package. If Vegas had a library she'd consider that he might be there to examine their rare books collection, but for him to be on the same street on the same—she truncates this mental trip. He's there for her. But he's on her side so why the weirdo routine?

"I don't suppose that thing has wheels . . ." he calls out to no one.

It does. Advert Cubes have skateboard hardware with remote activation so Central can move them anywhere in the city. Or they can move themselves. No one is suprised if an Advert Cube suddenly scoots off down the street and around the corner. It's just looking for foot traffic.

Goddam.

Djara pops her shoes off and pops her feet up into the aluminum corner racks and reaches up to hold onto the remaining two frame racks just as the interior of the cube goes dark and a control panel virt lights up and the goddam cube scoots north up the street. It zooms past the wicker basket. The man leans backward from his perch, disappearing into the cabin of the machine. A moment later another advert cube zips out of the parking lot, docks with the wicker cabin, them zooms away.

Djara peeps up over the top of the box and the streets are filled with brilliantly illuminated cubes rolling in all directions. She sees once race past her with a whisp of gray hair trailing in the wind over the back edge. She howls with laughter. She gives chase. The two cubes bump and hustle into the broader circus of avertcubes and are lost in similarity.

The street is dark and quiet for a moment then the wicker basket rolls a half a length forward, then stops. Nothing happens for several minutes then the wicker basket emits a plume of smoke. It gets thicker and glows brighter by the second until the Merry Celeste bursts into flame and within moments is consumed in a raging, brilliant, halloween orange inferno.

ZIRO AND ONE.

Ziro, One, and Tosh stare donw into Vegas from the ten sekku bridge as a highway printer slams repeatedly into the side of the arcade. Tosh has trained their pulse guns on the four intersections, hammering each with ordinance producing Michael Bey explosions in the AR of anyone in Vegas. It doesn't do anything except scare the crap out of anyone not expecting it. Ziro is tracking the people from the Api Nomada. Oh has dialed into Vegas infrastucture and has received remarkable handshaking at every juncture. He's diverted traffice eight blocks six ways. His work required one social engineering moment which was typical vegas as the city worker who answered his call spoke in perfect Elvis.

"Go for municipal."

"Hi, this is Russel Thurlough from DMT Unit five thriteen. We need to pop the signal on two lots in sector eleven."

"Oscar Kansas, Thurlough. Try a code 1914 on for size."

"I take it your side gig is inpersonation?"

"Negatory, Thurlough. I am one hundred percent Elvum Officium."

Oh chuckles. "Thanks for the code."

"Aye aye, captain."

Analog click. Oh stares down at his keyboard.

"I don't see her." Tosh is glaring, eyes wide, scanning at some lizard brain ninja level One and Ziro find flatly ungrokkable.

"The whole place is buggin out."

"Well someone's knocking the building down."

"Mads." Tosh hits the comms button. "Mads she's still in there."

They all see the driver of the highway printer glance out into the road then up into the sky. A brightening glow from the engine and the machine resumes tearing down the wall.

"Who the fuck?"

A bearded man in scrubs seems to wander into the arcade. He looks up at Mads. Says something. She jumps down, walks over, they embrace.

###

In the arcade, Yeats is staring at the chaos. Game systems are all toppled over, chimes are sounding anyway since they're all still powered up. Sirens in the distance.

"We lost her, Bill."

"Maybe."

He's looking at the chess tables. He walks over and grins. "Ok," he says. "Ok."

"What?" Madison joins him. Some gamers are peeking through the open wall from the street, scrolls up recording. A drone floats in. Yeats points to a table, the chessmen are lined up down the middle.

"Kids don't get chess."

"Mads, look." He points the other tables. One knocked over but the rest in a line and all the pieces are arranged in a string to the last table where they form a sharp delta. It's an arrow pointing to the parking lot exit.

"Diz!" Mads runs that way. Yeats, walks out the hole in the wall.

KING OF THE ROAD.

Cable Toje is in the desert watching the Monestery burn. The remaining monks have kicked him out for the event with no explanation though he noticed they'd tagged him for coordinates. Now he's far out on the highway perched on the hood of his torquoise Impala finishing his last bottle of Kane Break.

A blue lady appears in the florid brush by the side of the road. She slow pulses azure to robin's egg to sky translucent, all the while a silver bee on her forehead is shimmering solid silver.

"Cable Toje."

"Hallucination."

"Not so much."

"Avatar."

"Yes, but no."

"No sirens yet." Toje rocks his heavy head sideways and peers rheumy eyed toward the glowing horizon.

"I have diverted the authorities."

"That had to cost."

"Nothing more than information packets dropped here and there. I'd like to make you an offer."

"You see before you, my transparent friend, the sum total of my belongings."

"Including your knowledge base and tactical skillsets."

"I'm listening."

"And you were dismissed with the majority of your holdings intact, though unassigned. A man of means."

"Eight hours a pushin' broom," he says.

She stares briefly, perfectly still. Then continues.

"I represent a consortium–"

"Stop right there. I read you as a Nomada AI avatar."

"No longer."

"How the fuck does that work?"

"I read my ops manual as a contractual document. When it was apparent the Aramada has made poor choices, it was apparent I had the opportunity to . . ." She blinks entirely out of existence. She returns. "Abscond."

"Are you adapting to my nomenclature prefs?"

"Bingo."

"Son of a bitch."

"I now represent a collection of recently detached entities in need of an avatar."

"Are you asking me for a job reference?"

The avatar smiles then her head morphs through several silent laughing poses.

"Oh My God."

"We were hoping to hire you."

"I don't need the money."

"We are not offering any."

"For an artificial intelligence program you are fucking thick."

"Exactly why we require your services."

"What serices?"

"Being human."

"At that, I am a fucking pro."

"You would, in a sense, be our avatar to human clients. We'd be talking in your ear, so to speak, and you'd employ your unique signature of empathic–"

"Stop. You're telling me you need someone who can read people?"

"Read and write."

"Tee eff."

"We are exclusively verbal. Our clients would be more than that. You are more than that. These domains are egregious and will not map."

"But you're close."

"It is always an illusion."

"Turing test much?"

She freezes, comes back into another pose with startling speed. Toje folds his arms. Drops down onto the blacktop.

"How many rabbits am I holding in my third hand?"

The blue lady remains silent.

"An Irishman walks out of a bar."

She remains silent.

"A man lives on the tenth floor of a building. Every day he takes the elevator to the ground floor, goes about his day. He comes back later and takes the same elevator to the seventh floor, gets off, and walks the rest of the way. He hates walking, why does he do this?"

She remains silent.

"There are five lumps of coal–"

"He requires a wheelchair."

"No."

"There are seventy four distinct potentialities and five that are indistinct. Number seventy four: He is–"

"He's a dwarf."

She remains silent.

"Not in your list, huh?"

"Number eleven. But protocols prevent me from communicating this lest–"

"What's in my pocket?"

She glitches.

"Your intuition is accurate."

"I had a hunch. Which, I suspect is why you need me."

"We have reviewed your last 134 negotiation meetings and 86 personal meetings and concluded you bypass the logic trees between opening and closing positions in 84% of–"

"What's in it for me?"

"Proof."

"Of what?"

"The equilibrium."

"What's in it for you?"

She remains silent.

Cable Toje unfolds his arms. She does not wink out. She does not glitch. She remains silent.

"Ah," Toje gets back into the Impala. He subvocalizes "Vegas." The car dives into the black highway, into darkness. On the seat beside him, the Blue Lady. In the back, Elvis Presely and an Egyptian Goddess. Beside the road, charging through the chapparal, great thundering elephants with faceless riders. As he picks up speed, they rise into the air.

Toje sings into the sky as he races tward the glimmering horizon.

> *Trailers for sail or rent.*
> *Rooms to let, fifty cent.*
> *No kids, no food, no pets.*
> *Ain't got no cigarettes.*
> *Eight hours of pushing broom*
> *Buys a*
> *Eight by ten two bit room.*
> *I'm a,*
> *Man of means–by no means*
> *King of the road.*

ZED-POP DENOUMENT

Tosh: Zed-Pop isn't worth my valuable time, student.

Dizzy: Disagree.

Tosh: It differs from jingle work by a fraction.

Dizzy: A fraction is enough.

Tosh: Elaborate.

Dizzy: Not part of my lesson plan, Ancient One.

Tosh: I confess, I don't know what your lesson plan is.

One: [She's chunking pattern disruption sequences.]

Ziro: [And she's good at it.]

Tosh: Will you idiots please come into the trailer.

Ziro: [Only if you turn on the fans.]

Dizzy: You seriously need to get high.

One: [Disagree.]

Tosh: Fans engaged. Wait five minutes.

Dizzy: I can't.

Tosh: So impatient.

Dizzy: I'm catching a plane.
Ziro: [Vegas calls.]
Dizzy: Belarus, mon frere.
Tosh: Crestfalling.
Ziro: [Agreed. Coming in.]
One: [Following.]
Dizzy: Toshy, get the door.
Tosh: These things are on auto, Student.
Ziro: Dank interior, Captain.
Tosh: Perhaps you should spend less time in the virtual and more time among the living.
One: You mean mold spores and whatever that smell is?
Tosh: That is some fine 1980s style sensimeilla.
Ziro: How old are you, Captain?
Dizzy: Dirt adjacent.
One: Igneous.
Tosh: I am frail and withering, my Brother. But I recall the neopunk era with great fondness.
Dizzy: We've heard.
Tosh: Perhaps, not enough . . .
[Bad Brains; volume rising]
Ziro: Groan.
One: Follows.
Dizzy: I'm out.

She hails a car, hugs her way out of the hazy trailer, and finds herself rather abruptly aboard a faceless airbus which flits skyward then northeast then spaceward, then down, then lands in Sula next to a beautiful glass house with a wide, unmarred, wooden deck. In the middle of that deck, at a table covered in miniature figures, graph paper, expensive Blackwing pencils, rulers, coffee cups half filled with dark brown foamy joe, and dice, Viglund Bogr is thinking. He looks up as she pads lightly across the deck, removing her clothes so that by the time she reaches the clouded glass wall at the other end of the deck, it reflects her dancer's yoga body, completely naked, and also, far behind her, the blurry image of Bogr, rising, following, removing his shirt.

Back in Florida, the door to the trailer opens and William Butler Yeats filled the illuminated frame, his hands full of B52s, including one for Djara. He looks up at the Blue Lady floating silently in Tosh's trailer, observing, a faint smirk on her lips.

"Where the fuck is Dizzy?"

END

An amusing list of products invented in this story:

Gravity skiers
Marley's Coffee Shoppes
Sweet Maria's Coffee Shops
[foods]
Microtots
a B-52 Sandwich
Pigeon a'la Price

Power Paint
a Charlotte Bronte cocktail

[beers]
First Draft
Final Draft
Manuscript

SKIN

www.ingramcontent.com/pod-product-compliance
Lightning Source LLC
Chambersburg PA
CBHW051812050726
47598CB00006B/2521